How hum...
to her fi...
ripe old age of twenty-seven.

But then again, this was Miracle Harbor, Brittany thought. What if it was *him* at the door. The *one*. Her own Prince Charming to escort her to the ball, and through life ever after.

She opened the door, her breath stopping in her throat at the man who stood there. *"You."*

Was *he* going to show up every single time she contemplated wedded bliss? Did that mean something?

He looked down at her, and for a moment she was so mesmerized by his eyes that she was frozen. They were a shade of blue that reminded her of a sleepy ocean on a hot day.

"I'm Mitch Hamilton," he said, in *that* voice.

A voice that could make a perfectly proper girl like her think very naughty thoughts of what *exactly* it meant being married....

Dear Reader,

I'm dreaming of summer vacations—of sitting by the beach, dangling my feet in a lake, walking on a mountain or curling up in a hammock. And in each vision, I have a Silhouette Romance novel, and I'm happy. Why don't you grab a couple and join me? And in each book take a look at our Silhouette Makes You a Star contest!

We've got some terrific titles in store for you this month. Longtime favorite author Cathie Linz has developed some delightful stories with U.S. Marine heroes and *Stranded with the Sergeant* is appealing and fun. Cara Colter has the second of her THE WEDDING LEGACY titles for you. *The Heiress Takes a Husband* features a rich young woman who's struggling to prove herself—and the handsome attorney who lends a hand.

Arlene James has written over fifty titles for Silhouette Books, and her expertise shows. *So Dear to My Heart* is a tender, original story of a woman finding happiness again. And Karen Rose Smith—another popular veteran—brings us *Doctor in Demand*, about a wounded man who's healed by the love of a woman and her child.

And two newer authors round out the list! Melissa McClone's *His Band of Gold* is an emotional realization of the power of love, and Sue Swift debuts in Silhouette Romance with *His Baby, Her Heart,* in which a woman agrees to fulfill her late sister's dream of children. It's an unusual and powerful story that is part of our THE BABY'S SECRET series.

Enjoy these stories, and make time to appreciate yourselves in your hectic lives! Have a wonderful summer.

Happy reading!

Mary-Theresa Hussey

Mary-Theresa Hussey
Senior Editor

Please address questions and book requests to:
Silhouette Reader Service
U.S.: 3010 Walden Ave., P.O. Box 1325, Buffalo, NY 14269
Canadian: P.O. Box 609, Fort Erie, Ont. L2A 5X3

The Heiress Takes a Husband

CARA COLTER

SILHOUETTE *Romance*

Published by Silhouette Books

America's Publisher of Contemporary Romance

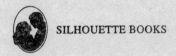

SILHOUETTE BOOKS

ISBN 0-373-19538-9

THE HEIRESS TAKES A HUSBAND

Visit Silhouette at www.eHarlequin.com

Printed in U.S.A.

CARA COLTER

shares ten acres in the wild Kootenay region of British Columbia with the man of her dreams, three children, two horses, a cat with no tail and a golden retriever who answers best to "bad dog." She loves reading, writing and the woods in winter (no bears). She says life's delights include an automatic garage door opener and the skylight over the bed that allows her to see the stars at night.

She also says, "I have not lived a neat and tidy life, and used to envy those who did. Now I see my struggles as having given me a deep appreciation of life, and of love, that I hope I succeed in passing on through the stories that I tell."

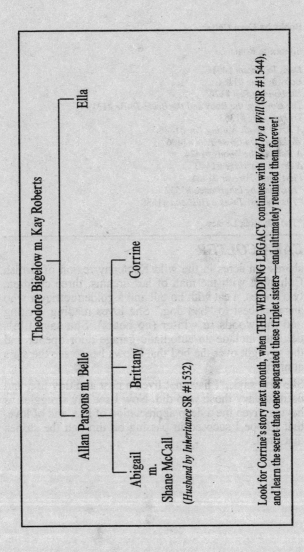

Theodore Bigelow m. Kay Roberts

Allan Parsons m. Belle

Abigail
m.
Shane McCall
(*Husband by Inheritance* SR #1532)

Brittany

Corrine

Ella

Look for Corrine's story next month, when THE WEDDING LEGACY continues with *Wed by a Will* (SR #1544), and learn the secret that once separated these triplet sisters—and ultimately reunited them forever!

Prologue

February 15

Brittany Patterson, who considered herself to be unshockable, was in shock.

It was everything she could do to keep her hands calmly folded on her lap, instead of wrapping her arms around herself and hugging, hard and long. It was everything she could do to keep the hot tears that smoldered behind her eyes from falling.

Sisters.

She, who had always been alone, was no longer alone.

Brittany wanted to scoff at her own sentiment. She hadn't been alone, precisely. She'd had her adoptive parents. Friends.

And yet when she glanced again at the faces of her sisters, so eerily similar to her own, she felt as if she had been lonely all her life, her heart waiting for something it knew.

Not just sisters. But triplets. Brittany Patterson had just found out she was one of triplets. She wanted to gaze at them, drink in their features, marvel at the quirk of Abby's mouth, Corrine's toss of her hair, mannerisms she possessed herself.

Instead, she forced herself to listen to the silver-haired Jordan Hamilton, hoping the lawyer would say something that would unravel the mystery of why they had not always been together.

Instead the mystery deepened.

He did not know why they had grown up apart, each unaware of the existence of the others. He knew only that they had been reunited, here, in his office by a person he would not name. And that same person had bestowed a gift on each of them.

Vaguely she registered her sister, Abby, had received a house. Vaguely she registered conditions. And then her own name penetrated the warm, misty fog of her brain, and she listened, some part of her alert, while the other still swam in the warmth of her discovery. Sisters.

"...the gift of the Main Street Bakery, 207 Main Street, Miracle Harbor, Oregon, on the condition that Miss Patterson reside in Miracle Harbor for a period of one year, and that she marry within that time period."

Brittany drew in her breath sharply, landed solidly on Planet Earth, and eyed the distinguished, silver-haired lawyer, waiting for him to laugh.

But he wasn't laughing.

"Mr. Hamilton, my parents are behind this, aren't they?" she said. She supposed they were regretting that they had taken such a firm stand after her car accident. They probably had found out, somehow, she had sold the beautiful Fabergé tennis bracelet just last week. In a way, their plot was brilliant.

"Your parents?" Jordan Hamilton asked. He seemed genuinely astonished.

"You know," she said, "buy me a career and get me

married off in one fell swoop." She said this lightly, as if it didn't matter one little bit to her that her parents did not think she was capable of looking after herself. Not that that assessment would be completely unfair.

Six months had passed since they had cut the purse strings, right after she had wrecked her beautiful apple-red Corvette and wound up in the hospital. Their terms were brutally simple. No allowance, no loans, no credit cards, no access to the bank account. They had told her they were not going to pay for her to kill herself, that it was time for her to join the real world, learn to be a responsible adult, make her contribution to the human race.

Six months, and Brittany had yet to find a job. Even though she was trying so hard.

"But what about us?" one of her sisters, Corrine, asked. "How could your parents manufacture us?"

"Why would *your* adoptive parents give me a house?" Abby chimed in.

Brittany started, and looked again at the other two women in the room. It was the strangest and somehow the loveliest feeling she had ever had.

She smiled, amazed at how much relief she felt that her adoptive parents weren't behind the fact she was sitting in this lawyer's office. Couldn't possibly be behind it.

"I guess," she said thoughtfully, "not even Mr. and Mrs. Conroy Patterson are rich enough to clone people. Not that I think they'd want to clone me."

"Why not?" Abby, the one in the navy blue dress that looked like something a nun would choose, asked with mild indignation.

So, Brittany thought, and nestled deeper into the warmth creeping through her, this is what it meant to have a sister. Abby didn't even know her, and it was evident she chose to believe the best of her, anyway.

But about getting married—

The door to the lawyer's office whispered open behind her. Brit glanced over her shoulder, and felt her eyes widen.

If *that's* what appeared when you even thought about getting married in a place called Miracle Harbor, then she was all for it, after all.

He was gorgeous. The proverbial tall—at least six feet of him—dark—crisp black hair and olive-tinted skin—and handsome—slanting brows, straight nose, sensual lips and strong chin. Add to that the fact that his conservative clothing did nothing to hide a lean body that rippled with easy male strength.

Then she noticed his eyes and felt her heart would tumble from her chest. They glittered wickedly, an impossible shade of blue, almost aquamarine, framed in a sooty abundance of spiky lashes.

Those eyes met hers, and held, coolly professional, and yet just beneath that look lurked something else. Something wildly intriguing…a hint of the untamed, a suggestion of potent male strength, a shadow of leashed sensuality.

In fact, despite the impeccable cut of the white linen shirt, rolled up at the sleeves, the silk tie, loosened slightly, she thought he'd look very at home with those long, muscled legs wrapped around a big black, silver-chromed engine-growling motorcycle, or a plunging wild-eyed stallion or—

She felt the heat rising in her cheeks, and looked swiftly away from him.

"My son," Jordan Hamilton murmured by way of introduction, "Mitch."

"Dad, I just have the Phillips' contract I need your signature on."

His voice was like raw silk caressing heated skin, and Brit shivered as if he had touched her. She felt almost panicked by the attraction she felt to him, curbed her urge to drink him in, and studied her fingernails instead until he had left the room.

"Now," the elder Mr. Hamilton said apologetically, "about the bakery..."

She tried to keep her mind from wandering out of the room with the intriguing younger Mr. Hamilton. Frankly a bakery wasn't even remotely close to what Brittany was looking for. Something in public relations had seemed more her line, or marketing. Or being the buyer for a posh clothing store. Something like that. A fun job where she had an expense account and a clothing allowance and flew to Paris and Milan on a regular basis.

But since not one of the companies where she had applied for such positions had even had the courtesy to call her back, she'd have to use a dumb bakery to show everyone just what she could do, to live up to the faith in her that she saw shining in her sisters' eyes.

An hour later, she was walking arm and arm with her sisters, reveling in the looks of delighted surprise they attracted from the citizens of Miracle Harbor as they sashayed down the main street.

A main street out of a picture book. White-capped waves crashing against a sandy shore on one side of the street, lovely old brick buildings, with colorful awnings lining the other.

"This won't be such a terrible place to spend a year," she decided, out loud. "It's cute and quaint. Perfectly adorable. And being here with you, with my sisters, and getting a chance to know you..." she sighed happily without finishing the sentence.

"You seem to be forgetting the husband part," Corrine pointed out, sourly. Corrine was dressed in blue jeans with a rip in the knee and a denim jacket faded nearly white.

"Oh, pooh, people get married all the time for less than

romantic reasons. I doubt any of the couples my parents know got married because they loved each other. Certainly my parents didn't.'' Nothing in her tone of voice revealed a little girl who had ached for authentic love, the only gift her wealthy parents had seemed incapable of giving.

''I think that's sad,'' Abby said softly, just as if she had glimpsed that little girl despite Brittany's carefully measured tone.

''It's realistic,'' Brittany said quickly, and added with a devilish wink, ''If I like my bakery, I'll put an ad in the paper—Husband Wanted. Must be tall, dark and handsome. Something like that gorgeous lawyer who came into the office to get something signed. What was his name?''

As if she would ever forget. But if Brit had a talent it was for not letting people know exactly what she really felt, a talent for never being too vulnerable. It seemed to her it might be unnecessary to protect herself from her sisters, but on the other hand, old habits died hard, and in this one area she always chose to err on the side of caution.

''I think it was Mike,'' Corrine said.

''No, it wasn't,'' Abby corrected her. ''Mark.''

''Well, definitely an *M*,'' Brit said, secretly delighted that neither of her sisters had apparently seen him as a prospect.

''I'll move here for a year to get to know both of you,'' Corrine said, ''but I can't just drop everything and come. It will be at least May before I can get here. And I'm not getting married because someone tells me I have to. Forget it.''

''I'll help you find a husband you like,'' Brittany said cheerfully, ''but first we'll have to lose the jeans. You'd look wonderful in Ralph Lauren because,'' she giggled, ''I do.''

And then she laughed at Corrine's dark expression. She squeezed her hand, and was rewarded with a small smile that allowed her to glimpse the sweetness of her sister Corrine's spirit.

It seemed to Brittany that Abby and Corrine's love was wrapping around her, an unconditional gift she had done nothing to earn, and it was as soft as the fragrant mist off the sea.

She felt she had never been so happy, so full of hope, so excited about life and all its wonderful possibilities.

She looked up at the bronze numbers over the businesses, and felt herself holding her breath. 201, 203, 205...

Then, she saw the bakery. Her bakery.

Chapter One

Two months later...

"Just a minute," Brittany called, when the knock came on her apartment door, again. She looked in the full-length mirror in her bedroom, oblivious to the unmade bed, the scattered clothing, the open makeup pots.

"I look awful," she wailed. "Awful."

The knock came again, firm, unrelenting. She ignored it.

It was hopeless. The bridesmaid's dress was peach chiffon. Sleeveless, it fit her like a dream, swirled around her trim figure, showed off the slender length of her legs, the swell of her bosom, the curve of sun-kissed shoulders. The dress was perfect.

And her makeup was perfect, too. Her high cheekbones accentuated, the blue-gold of her eyes shown off, her lips looking dewy and wet, her skin golden peach.

Her long hair, expertly highlighted so that it glittered with threads of gold and wheat and honey, was piled up on top of her head, just the odd wild tendril allowed to escape.

She looked absolutely stunning, in every way, and it was spoiled, totally ruined by one disastrous detail. Paint.

Pink paint.

A thick stripe of it ran through the gold strands of her hair, and speckles of the same shade were scattered over her bare arms from wrists to shoulders. Nothing would convince it to go. And she knew, because she had tried everything from paint thinner to nail polish remover.

It was the result of repainting the interior of her bakery, without question the most grueling labor she had ever done. She had chosen an absolutely posh shade of pink. Okay, after four whole days of doing nothing but working with it, it was not nearly as appealing as she found it at first, but that was perfectly understandable.

And she *really* didn't care for it as a fashion accessory, but she reminded herself firmly, no sacrifice was too great to make for her bakery, and for her successful entrance into the Miracle Harbor business community. She had been given a brand-new chance. A brand-new life, really, and what was a little pink paint in the face of that?

Bang, bang, bang.

If whoever that was didn't quit knocking on the door, she was going to scream. Except maybe successful business people weren't allowed to scream.

She'd settle for leveling them with a look, whoever was at her door, impertinently ignoring her request for just a little more time. No doubt it was the escort, rounded up for her by her sister, Abby. With the bakery reopening next week, Brit simply never had enough time anymore for anything.

So, how had Abby found time between her seamstress job, *and* raising a baby, *and* getting married to find a date for her sister for the wedding?

Given Abby's schedule, Brit thought it would be unreasonable on her part to expect much for an escort. How humiliating, at the ripe old age of twenty-seven, being subjected to her first blind date. How dreadful that for her first Miracle Harbor social outing her companion for the evening might be less than stellar. Old. Ugly. What if he was wrinkled?

On the other hand, this was Miracle Harbor.

Look what had happened to Abby.

What if the very same thing happened to her? What if, within a week of arriving here, Brit met *him*. The *one*. Her very own Prince Charming to escort her to the ball, and through life ever after.

With one last resigned glance in the mirror, and one more sigh about the paint, she whirled and moved determinedly in the direction of her front door. She tried not to notice how humble the furnishings of her apartment were, tried not to see them through the eyes of her escort. Her place was an apartment above the bakery and it had come furnished. On her best days she could see that as a blessing, on her worst she hated to think about the rump that had left that worn dent on the fading sofa.

"Oh," she muttered to herself, "he'll probably be too decrepit and wrinkled to even notice anything beyond me." *And my pink paint,* she added wryly to herself.

He banged again. The click of her high heels might have conveyed just a touch of her impatience, but she pasted a cool smile on her face before she flung open her front door.

"I said just a min—" her voice stopped in her throat. *"You."*

Was he going to show up every single time she contemplated wedded bliss? Did that mean something?

It meant the pink paint, and the furniture *mattered*.

She stepped out onto the narrow wooden landing with the delightful view of Main Street's back alley, and pulled the door mostly closed behind her.

He looked down at her, and for a moment she was so

mesmerized by his eyes that she was frozen. They were a shade of blue that reminded her of a sleepy ocean on a hot day.

"I'm Mitch Hamilton," he said, in *that* voice, a voice that could make a perfectly proper girl like her think very naughty thoughts of exactly what being married meant.

It meant his lips and his hands claiming her, holding her, owning her. It meant that deep voice in her ear growling incredible endearments. It meant waking up to his face every single morning, the sharp hollows of his cheeks shadowed with whiskers.

"Mitch Hamilton," he said again, faintly bemused.

She drew herself up short, stunned at where her thoughts had gone, stunned by the force of the attraction, stunned to see *nothing* reciprocated in those ocean eyes.

Miracle Harbor or not, she decided, she was not making a fool of herself over any man.

"Pleased to meet you," she said formally, diamond-edged ice in her voice.

Still, despite the small victory over her voice, she could not look away. It wasn't just that he was compellingly handsome, or that *he,* of course, looked unnervingly perfect, in a navy blue suit with a fine pinstripe. Custom tailored, she guessed, to encompass the immense broadness of those shoulders. He had on a crisp white silk shirt, that made his skin look bronze and sun-warmed, a dark tie, the knot perfect and square. His legs were long, the slacks just hinted at the ridged cut of a very muscular thigh.

He looked every inch the successful man. Still, for all that sophistication, for all the obvious expense of the suit, she still saw it there. A glint in those amazing eyes that hinted at a part of him untamed. Perhaps even untamable?

Inwardly, she wondered how Abby could do this to her. She suddenly found herself wishing for what had moments ago seemed like it would be her worst nightmare. Someone old and wrinkled and ugly.

A man she could handle with one arm tied behind her back, *and* several gallons of paint splashed over herself.

But this man…he was a man out of a dream. Handsome. Well-made. Oozing male confidence and subtle sensuality. He was the kind of man who simply took a woman's breath away, made her go weak with strange and forbidden longings.

And she had pink paint in her hair, and reptilian spots all over her arms. Which, to give her credit, Abby didn't know about.

Yet.

"How could she do this to me?" she murmured, to herself, but out loud this time. She gave her head a rueful shake, hoping to clear the spell she was floundering under and become herself. Cosmopolitan. Sophisticated. Witty. In control.

"Pardon?" He took a step back and glanced hopefully for an apartment number, as if he were suddenly wishing he was in the wrong place.

There was no number. Hers was just one set of stairs in a long line of them that came up from the back lane to the stuffy little apartments located over the main street businesses.

"Are you Brittany? Brittany Patterson?"

"Unfortunately."

"I'm sorry. Who did what to you?" He cocked an eyebrow at her, tilted his head.

"My sister. You."

"My father, Jordan Hamilton, asked me if I would escort you to your sister's wedding," he said with a certain stiff dignity.

She realized he had been roped into the task of escorting

her to Abby's wedding. And that he obviously was not nearly as swayed by her, as she was by him.

Adjectives kept running through her head, as she gazed helplessly at him. Gorgeous. Stunning. Dazzling.

Because she wanted more than anything else for him to *want* to take her to her sister's wedding. And because that made her feel weak and silly, and the way she least liked to feel—vulnerable—she said, "I'm sure everyone's intentions were great, but I certainly don't need an escort. I'm quite happy to go by myself."

His eyes narrowed and she felt a funny shiver go down her spine as she recognized that his will was at least as strong as hers. Perhaps, heaven forbid, stronger.

"My orders are to get you to the church on time." He slid back an impeccable sleeve and glanced at a watch. A Rolex watch. "Which means we have to leave. Now."

She noticed again his voice, deep-timbred, even more sensual with that note of implacable sternness in it. But for all the smooth confidence of his voice that same hint of something wild ran at the edges of it.

Of course, the autocratic note she could do without.

With incredible effort she pulled herself together. That would be the day when she ever let a man like this get the upper hand, let him think she would allow herself to be bossed around like an errant child!

"Well, we can't leave right now," she said firmly. "I can't. I'm not ready."

This invited his inspection. He looked at her closely, his gaze suddenly uncomfortably intense, nothing in it suggesting he was coming up with a lovely list of adjectives to describe her.

"You look fine to me."

Fine?

"Except you seem to have," he reached out a tentative hand, and touched, "something in your hair. Bubble gum?"

She jerked away from his hand, appalled by the ridiculous sensation that electricity had shot from his fingertips.

"Paint! It's on my arms, too. This is unbelievable." That she was standing here talking to this ravishing man about *this*. "It will not come off. How can they manufacture something like that? Aren't there laws?"

"I'm afraid laws concerning paint products are not my specialty." His amusement was reluctant.

"What am I going to do?" she asked, more to herself than him.

"Hope for dim lighting," he suggested, without an appropriate amount of sympathy. "We have to go *now*."

"I can't. You don't understand." He really didn't understand, how important it was that today, of all days, she be absolutely faultless. And not for herself and not so he could see her at her ravishing best, though certainly that would have been a bonus.

"It's Abby's day," she whispered, "and it needs to be perfect. I'm a bridesmaid. I'll be in all the pictures. I can't wreck her pictures."

She had the funniest feeling that she had just revealed something more of herself than she was prepared to have rejected by his Royal Handsomeness, because he was looking at her closely as if he was seeing something he hadn't seen before.

"The pictures will probably be in that horrible little paper," she said swiftly. "I can't be seen like this."

His eyes became impatient, but his voice did not. "It doesn't look that bad. Bubble gum is obviously not your shade, but I really don't think it's that noticeable. Not like, say, neon green."

"Please stop calling it bubble gum. It's frosted dawn," she informed him regally.

"And how did, er, frosted dawn, end up on bleached blond?"

Bleached blond? She wasn't even going to dignify that by responding to it. This man knew how to make an enemy.

"I happen to be painting," she informed him in a chilled tone.

"An artist," he said, as if that explained all kinds of eccentricities. "The last show the museum brought in was done by a dog. Seriously. He had had his tail dipped in paint, and wagged it over the canvas."

The most handsome man she had ever, ever laid eyes on, had casually grouped her, the bleached blonde, in the same category as a dog that painted with its tail.

She sighed. She had looked forward to this day with eagerness and delight. It was the day of her sister's wedding, a day that confirmed miracles really did happen to the most ordinary of people, a day that celebrated love. A day that filled her with this wistful, secret hope that maybe one day, in the not too distant future, she too would be a bride.

Now, she could tell things were just not going to go exactly as per her plan. Anything close to her plan. For today. And that probably included the rest of her life, too.

"I'm not an artist!" she told him coldly. "I'm painting the walls. In my business."

He looked at the shade in her hair incredulously. "Really?"

"This shade looks much better on the walls."

"Really?" he said again. A slow smile was spreading across those firm lips, slow and warm and sexy.

How could Abby do this to her?

"It's not funny," she told him desperately.

"Of course not," he said, in a voice that could easily have tacked "Your Honor" on the end of his response. The smile disappeared. "But do you know what really wouldn't be amusing? Being late for the wedding. That *could* spoil the occasion. This, on the other hand," he gestured at her hair, ''will probably be a source of great amusement every time everyone looks at the pictures for years to come.''

''A source of amusement,'' she muttered unhappily. ''For years to come.''

Still she looked at her watch, and with a little cry of dismay knew he was right. She had to leave.

Apparently with him.

Giving him a look of regal dislike, as if he were responsible for the fact she had paint on her head, she swept by him and down her creaky steps.

''Why do I have the awful feeling this is going to be the worst evening of my life?'' she murmured as he had to reach out and grab her elbow when her ankle turned on the step.

''Ditto,'' he responded dryly, letting go of her arm with extreme and unnecessary haste.

She let him open the car door for her, a jet-black Mercedes 600SL, a car she had personally always considered more conceited than sporty.

He slid into his seat, and started the powerful engine, looking straight ahead, not even attempting conversation.

A soldier carrying out orders.

''You didn't want to do this, did you?''

He glanced at her, looked ahead again, and did not look the least uncomfortable. ''I did it as a favor to my father.''

''You must care a great deal about your father since its obvious you'd rather be eating raw jalapeño peppers chased down with chili sauce.''

He smiled slightly. ''I have great respect for my father, but it's true that given an option, I wouldn't exactly jump at an opportunity to spend an awkward evening with a total stranger.''

''It seems to me it could have been much worse,'' she snapped.

"Oh?"

"I could have been old. And wrinkled. And ugly."

He didn't say anything, his silence far more insulting than if he had responded.

"And you did have an option. I told you I was capable of going by myself."

"I didn't have an option," he said grimly. "I told my father I'd take you. And I will."

"I suspect you have hopelessly old-fashioned notions about honor and integrity," she said as if that were a bad thing.

When really it seemed to her she had discovered the most amazing of men.

Wasn't it just her luck that he was a man who had no intention of being "discovered"? Or at least not on a blind date, by a woman with pink hair, who lived at the top of a flight of rickety stairs. If only she could have made that all-important first impression count.

Brittany decided life was unbearably cruel.

Despite the melodrama of that thought, she found the wedding was beautiful once she got there, even with the paint in her hair, which nobody noticed, and the unwilling escort at her side, whom everybody did. Abby and Shane looked gloriously happy as they exchanged vows.

But the rest of the evening lived up to her dismal expectations.

Throughout dinner, Mitch Hamilton was a disapproving, humorless presence who defied her every effort to ignore him. She could still feel the sting of his disapproval over the story with which she'd entertained the other guests at their table.

A really funny story, about the one hundred and thirty-two packages of red food color she had put in her parents' pool at their home in Highwoods in California when she was a kid.

Mr. High-and-Mighty hadn't even laughed. He'd looked bored and then looked at his watch as if counting the minutes he'd have to put up with her.

Still, he had a certain physical allure—that same almost electrical sensation she had felt when he touched her hair— exuding from him, that made it impossible to pretend he did not exist.

Not that he was ever going to know it from her.

Now, the dance had started, and Brittany focused more intently on the couple who held center stage. Brittany was not sure she had ever seen such a beautiful sight.

Her sister, Abby, the train of her long ivory wedding dress held up from sweeping the floor by a lace loop attached to her wrist, was dancing her first dance as Mrs. McCall. She and her husband, Shane, moved around the room with the grace of two people who had been born to dance together.

There was something in the way they were looking at each other that made Brit want to believe all over again in possibility. Fairy tales. Happy endings. True love.

Her sister and her new husband danced as if they were alone in the room. The light that shone from their eyes combined wonder and tenderness and passion to such a degree it made a lump rise in Brittany's throat.

Be happy, she ordered herself sternly, taking another quick, soothing gulp of the champagne, especially when it felt like the tears pricking at the back of her eyes were going to fall. As if she'd ever cry in front of *him.*

"Did you want another glass of champagne?" His voice was ice and steel, tinged with an underlying disapproval, as if she were drinking too much.

Brit noticed, with some surprise, that her champagne glass *was* empty.

"Why not?" she said.

Her escort looked like he was debating giving her a few

reasons why not, then with a shrug snagged her a drink off a passing tray. None for him, though, Mr. Control.

"Loosen up," she told him. "Be happy. It's a wedding."

He studied her for a moment. "You don't look that happy."

"I am so," she said, taking another swig, recognizing just a touch of defiance in the gesture. Her sincerest wish was to be happy for her sister, but the truth was she felt envious.

It just wasn't fair. Her sister had been given a house. With a man in it. A gorgeous man, who had fallen hopelessly and helplessly in love with Abby in the space of weeks.

It just wasn't fair. Her sisters were the ones who had been appalled at the prospect of having to get married to retain their gifts.

Brittany had been the realistic one! Marriages were about gaining security or prestige or power. Love?

Abby had all the luck.

And I got a bakery.

"How is the bakery?" he asked.

She realized she had spoken out loud, and that maybe she should take it easy on the champagne. Having made that decision, she took another swig.

"Fine," she said, smiling with fake brightness. He had asked only to meet the minimum requirement for politeness. He didn't want to know the truth—that the bakery was a disaster. A little hole in the wall on main street, with aging equipment, horrible decor and no guy, unless she counted Luigi, the grouchy, middle-aged man who did the baking.

Still, in her better moments, she clung to its potential, was nearly dazzled with all the possibilities. Outdoor tables facing the ocean, a fuller menu, a French chef, famous artists vying for space on her walls...

His voice cut through her daydreams. "Did I notice it was closed last week?"

"I officially took over last week, and closed for a few days," she said. "I'm redecorating for the grand reopening on Monday."

When she had first sat in *her* bakery, with her sisters, at one of the six tiny little card tables, it had been so easy to dream. New floors, cute tablecloths, fresh flowers, pink paint, wallpaper. She hadn't really realized how *hard* it was to turn a simple dream into a tangible reality. But still, in a few days, the hard part would be over. And it would be worth it.

"Ah, the paint," he said. "What made you decide to tackle painting?"

Money seemed like too crass an answer, so she shrugged.

"You don't exactly seem like the handy type. Rollers and overalls, paint thinners. A hat."

She had never wanted to be the handy type, so why did it annoy her so much that he could see she wasn't? The hat was an unnecessary dig. She had thought of a hat, but didn't like the way hats flattened her hair.

"So what type do I look like?" she asked, tilting her chin up proudly.

"The Yellow Pages type."

Why did she feel so aggravated that he was seeing her so accurately? The truth was that's exactly what she would have been if she'd had the money to indulge herself. But when she'd phoned several painting companies, she'd been appalled at what they wanted to paint one little room. Her budget for the redecorating was a thousand dollars, the price she had gotten for her last piece of jewelry, a pair of beautiful emerald earrings set in platinum. There was no more jewelry to sell, which had been just about the most frightening feeling of her entire life.

If she didn't count that bottom-falling-out-of-her-world

feeling she was getting every time she took another sip of champagne and looked more deeply into his eyes.

She hadn't figured painting would be hard work. She'd actually entertained the notion it would be fun. It *had* been fun. For the first fifteen minutes.

"What made you choose bubble gum pink?" he asked.

"Frosted dawn!" she snapped, though the awful truth was that was exactly what the inside of her shop looked like—a bubble of gum that someone had exploded all over her walls. Between her inexpertise and the old surfaces of the walls, the paint had not taken evenly. In some places, where she had impatiently put the paint on too thick there were ghastly dribbles, teardrop shaped, down the walls. In others, where she had tried to do a second coat before the first one was dry enough, the paint looked rough and angry.

"Did you get *any* on the walls?" he asked.

She tilted her chin a little more, and wondered, just a little fuzzily, if he was laughing at her. "As a matter of fact, the walls look great." This was a lie. But she *knew* they would look great once she covered the worst of the mess with wallpaper and posters. Which meant tomorrow, Sunday, when the rest of the world would be sleeping in and frolicking on the beach with their families, she would be working. And it was darned hard work, especially for a girl who had never even cleaned her own bathroom.

"Well," he said, "just be thankful you didn't try wallpapering. An amateur can make a real mess of that."

"Really?" she said, and successfully hid her panic by taking another slug of champagne.

"What made you want to repaint? I thought it looked fine. My Dad and I go there for morning coffee most weekdays."

It occurred to her he was actually making conversation, probably only in an attempt to slow down her champagne consumption, which was really none of his business. Still, this was an improvement over icy, disapproving silence.

That little Cinderella hope inside her flared to life.

"The paint reflects a change in mood," she told him earnestly. His Dad and he came to the bakery. Why would she care that it wasn't one of the secretaries, that he wasn't meeting his girlfriend there?

"A moody bakery," he said, the finest edge of mockery in his voice.

"You'd be amazed what I'm planning on doing with that place."

His expression made her want to convince him, and the champagne loosened her tongue.

"I'm renaming it for starters. The Main Street Bakery. What does that say?"

"That it's on Main Street? That it's a bakery?"

"It says no imagination. Dull, dull, dull, is what it says. The new name is Heavenly Treats. Don't you think that plays well on the miracle part? Of Miracle Harbor?"

"I guess," he said doubtfully. "Though I'm not sure that's what people go to the bakery for. Miracles. I think they just want a loaf of bread, or a doughnut and coffee."

She ignored his pragmatism. What place did that have in the spinning of dreams? "I'm introducing specialty coffees, and some European-style treats. Doughnuts and coffee are so passé."

"Passé," he agreed. There was really no doubting the mocking edge to his voice now.

"There's a place in Los Angeles called The Chocolate Bar that sells specialty desserts for five dollars a pop!"

He still looked unimpressed.

"And of course, I'm going to get some little café-style tables, and put them outside, facing the beach. Red-checked tablecloths."

"That sounds interesting," he said, as if it sounded anything but.

"You don't think I'm going to be able to pull this off." She realized this suddenly, and felt deflated, and then annoyed with herself for caring what he thought.

"I never said that."

"I can tell what you're thinking."

"In that case, you might want to offer a little mind-reading business on the side. Madam Brittany. Do you do palms?"

"You're making fun of me." What was it with her? Did she have a big sign on her head that invited people not to take her seriously? Is that why she'd had no response to her job applications?

She'd show them all. Heavenly Treats was going to be a huge success. The painting might not be going as planned, but that was a minor glitch. The *real* job began when the bakery reopened on Monday.

She could already see herself, standing there in the nice little Caroline Herrera sundress with the keyhole neckline. She had decided ages ago it would be perfect for this occasion. She could picture herself greeting customers, telling them about the day's specialties, going from table to table at her outdoor café refilling cappuccino cups and taking orders for more slices of five-dollar tortes.

She could picture herself being admired for her panache, and her imaginative approach to business and her delightful light touches.

Not one single person would know she was scared to death.

"Are you scared?" he asked her, suddenly, regarding her with unsettling intensity.

"Scared?" She laughed. "Now who's playing at mind reader? You don't know the first thing about Brit Patterson, do you? And if anybody, including you, thinks I'm going to put my heart and soul into Heavenly Treats, and then lose it over a little detail like the fact I'm not married, they can think again.''

The speech, she realized would have been more effective without the embarrassing hiccup in the middle of it.

She managed to restrain herself from blurting out the rest of her plan. After all the hard work she'd already invested in the place, her ad was going in the paper next week. Husband Wanted.

''I think it's our turn.''

His voice was deep and sexy and full of authority. He was standing, his hand held out to her. He was such a commanding figure. He had loosened his tie, and she could see the strong column of his throat, the beginning of springy, dark hairs on his chest.

It would be nice if he was asking her to dance out of anything but a sense of duty, but of course that wasn't the case. The rest of the wedding party was joining the bride and groom on the dance floor.

Brittany put her hand in Mitch's.

Another shock of awareness shivered through her as his hand, warm and dry and infinitely strong, closed around hers.

A moment later they were on the dance floor. The band was playing a waltz.

He danced very properly. No pulling too tight and groping for him. A good-sized gorilla could have inserted itself in the space between them. She glanced up at his face. Remote. Nothing in it to suggest he shared her feeling of wanting to move a little closer, hold a little harder.

She decided, just a touch fuzzily, that it should be a criminal offense to be as good-looking as he was.

She would have to tell Abby, at some more opportune occasion, that this was the kind of surprise she did not need in a life that was already thoroughly and not always pleasantly surprising. Still, she supposed it was the kind of thing sisters did, and she knew Abby had meant well setting her up. But then who could have guessed he was such a grouch?

Mitch danced flawlessly, which did not surprise her. Everything about him would be flawless. He probably ironed his underwear.

Suddenly, she had to be looking anywhere but at him. What if he looked in her face and *saw* how hopelessly chaotic he made her thoughts? What if he saw that as effortlessly as he had seen she was scared?

"Lucky guess," she muttered.

"Pardon?"

"Lucky dress," she said. "The one my sister Corrine is wearing. She told me."

He looked like he thought she was drunk, which she wasn't. She was only the tiniest bit tipsy. He was the one making her act impaired. His presence, his hand intertwined with hers, the aroma coming off him of soap, and aftershave.

The attraction felt like a beast within her, leaping, hurling itself against a chain-link fence, frothing at the mouth, completely ignoring her feeble commands to get in control.

By now, if Mitch had an ounce of good old hot, red blood flowing in his veins, he really should have noticed how terrific she looked beyond the paint.

She decided, abruptly, that she had had it with Mitch Hamilton and his indifference to her considerable charms.

She felt cut to the quick, hurt beyond reason.

She wanted to tear herself away from him, run and hide in the bathroom. And then after everyone was gone, she could come out and limp home in her high-heeled shoes in the darkness.

Pathetic, she told herself. She would not be pathetic. Besides, if she did that, if she ran away and hid, he would know he could affect her. And she wasn't going to let him know that.

She knew she had to do the exact opposite of running away. Her life depended on it. Her whole sense of her self.

She closed the distance between them, pressed herself into the long length of his body. *Remain indifferent to that,* she challenged him silently.

At first he went very still, and then his hand found the small of her naked back and pressed her into him, yet closer. His body was somehow more than she had expected. Harder. She could feel the ridges of his muscles against her own softness.

She hadn't really expected this. To feel as if she had been born to dance with him as surely as Abby had been born to dance with Shane. She hadn't expected to feel powerless instead of powerful.

Stunned by the feelings shooting through her, and by how vulnerable and needy they made her feel, she committed more deeply and more desperately to convincing him the exact opposite was true.

She kissed him.

At first his lips, tasting of raindrops and honey, were motionless, absolutely still, beneath hers. She registered, in slow motion, how soft they felt, when they looked so hard.

Have some pride, she ordered herself, *pull away.*

But her lips mutinied and did exactly as they pleased. The beast howled happily within her. She wanted to taste Mitch, could not get enough of the taste of him, would forgo champagne forever in favor of this much headier blend. Her lips nudged his, slid across them, coerced, begged.

And when his lips answered, her world exploded, was annihilated. Her whole world became sensation, the touch of his lips on hers. Everything and everyone else faded.

They were alone, their world only this.

The kiss was like a rocket ignited, that soared heavenward and exploded into tiny fragments of delight. She could feel the fragments of that kiss float through her, until not one part of her was left untingling. Her whole body seemed to shake and shimmer, to take on an almost iridescent quality.

He pulled away first, and she stared up at him, dazed, shell-shocked from the abrupt transition from one world to the other. His blue eyes were dark and unreadable, but she could feel the faintest tremor, desire leashed, where his hand rested on the small of her back.

She laughed, shakily. She'd blown it. How could he remain unaware that he affected her after that?

He did not return her smile.

Lightly, she said, "How much do you know about the gifts my sisters and I are receiving?"

"Enough."

You're playing with fire, her mind warned her, but the champagne kept her going.

Why not him? She needed a husband, and he could kiss like a house on fire. That could certainly make up for his lack of a sense of humor. She could ask carelessly, she could appear not to be the least concerned about his answer.

"You might want to think about the conditions of my receiving my gift."

"Conditions?" he asked, his voice smooth and unperturbed, those ocean foam eyes unsettling in their steadiness on her face.

"You know what I'm talking about."

"Living in Miracle Harbor for a year?"

"No," she said.

"Oh, the other condition."

She inclined her head slightly, waited.

He smiled, so slow and sexy it felt like it could make
her bones melt. He leaned close to her.

And said, quietly, his breath tickling the nape of her
neck, ''Not if you were the last woman on earth.''

Chapter Two

For a moment, Mitch thought he'd gone too far.

His "not if you were the last woman on earth" hung in the sudden silence between them.

For a moment, she didn't seem like some glorious goddess of light and fire and passion. But then all that confidence seemed to crumple, as if it had been an illusion.

In the blink of an eye, she looked young and vulnerable, and like a child who had had her hand slapped for reaching for the candy. *Him. Candy?*

He must have been kidding himself, because the look left her eyes almost instantly, if it had been there at all.

Then she smiled brilliantly, and said, "Isn't it a good thing for me, I have a Plan B?"

"I'm afraid to ask."

She tossed her hair and leaned toward him. "I'm putting an ad in the newspaper."

"For a husband?" Too late he realized she *wanted* to shock him.

She nodded cheerfully.

"I don't think that's a very wise thing to do." It wasn't what he wanted to say. He wanted to take her by her slender shoulders, give her a shake and tell her not to be so bloody stupid.

But he didn't want to touch her again. Her skin had been like silk under his fingertips, and touching her had made him feel a helpless and nameless longing. It had made him feel weak, almost defenseless against her, and he hated that feeling enough that he intended to fight it with everything he had. And that was before she had kissed him.

Which is why he had told her he wouldn't marry her if she was the last woman on earth. He wasn't surrendering to her power. No doubt every man she had ever met had capitulated to her potent brand of charm, but he wasn't going to.

He should mind his own business about her ad, too. He didn't want to look like he cared about what foolishness she got into. Dammit. He did not care.

How could he care? He knew nothing about her beyond the few details in her case file. The adopted only child of Mr. and Mrs. Conroy Patterson, aging California jet-setters. Brit Patterson up close and personal appeared to be all that the file had implied: a spoiled, self-centered rich girl who was getting an unwelcome taste of real life.

Okay, so she happened to be so beautiful he felt like he couldn't breathe around her.

And she happened to pack a kiss with more punch than a trainload full of TNT.

He felt a tap on his shoulder, and turned to see Farley Houser, another lawyer from his firm, cutting in. Cutting in. Mitch didn't even know that happened in real life. He thought it only happened in movies, which probably said all that needed saying about his social life.

Why did he feel so annoyed? He should be glad to be out of her clutches.

He stood there for a moment, watching her laugh up into Farley's handsome, if somewhat sun-damaged face. What if she thought wrinkles were distinguished?

What did he care what she thought? Farley, who seemed to work for amusement and not because he needed money, would probably be a perfect match for her. Meeting him here could save her some money on her newspaper ad. Farley loved getting married. That's why he had done it three times.

Still, Mitch had to ask himself if he sincerely wished Brit and Farley well, why was he gauging how Farley held her, ready to intervene in an instant if the space between their bodies closed, as if he were a chaperone at the high school dance?

Mitch joined his father and Angela Pondergrove at their table. But if he had hoped his father would talk business with him, and therefore take his mind off the intoxicating kiss he had just shared with Brittany Patterson, he was wrong.

Jordan Hamilton was embarrassingly enamored with the aging Angela. He spared Mitch only a few words before he turned his full attention back to his companion. When he leaned close and called her "Angel," Mitch had no choice but to find something else to do with his eyes. He watched with relief as the music changed tempo from a waltz to some rock tune he recognized only vaguely.

He glanced around. Every male eye was on Brittany. His relief died. The girl could dance. She moved with grace and a subtle promise of sensuality. Her laughter floated on the air, like the tinkling of fairy bells. Farley, Mitch noted glumly, was an exceptional dancer, as well. The music died, and Farley, regret all over his face, gave her up to the Higgins boy who roasted hotdogs at the Piggy-in-A-Blanket stand during the day, and looked surprisingly like John Travolta by night.

After several dances it occurred to Mitch she was not going to return to their table. The local guys were around her three thick, like bees around honey.

What now? Could he go home? He didn't think Jordan would approve of him abandoning his duties as her escort. The truth was Jordan didn't ask many favors of him. And yet Mitch owed this man everything. Maybe he could look at sitting here at this dance, steam threatening to come out his ears, as part of his repayment to a man who had taken a wild, angry boy off the streets and given him a home, a life, a career.

So, he sat there, his mood getting darker and darker, as he watched the endless whirl of activity around her. It didn't even seem to put a dent in her energy.

It was two in the morning before she made her way back to him. Angela and Jordan had long since departed. Brit's face was glowing with laughter, looking as good as she had looked the moment he had first seen her. Better. Flushed. Exhilarated. Her bosom heaving delicately under the clinging fabric of that dress. She was absolutely at home with being the center of male attention and the belle of the ball.

"Mitch, there you are!"

He had barely changed position all evening, except to shed his jacket and tie, and roll up his sleeves against the insufferable heat in the room.

"I hope you weren't waiting for me," she said breathlessly. "Farley has offered to take me home." She leaned confidentially closer to him. "He thinks the pink stripe in my hair is so cute. He said I could start a trend."

"I don't think so," Mitch said, standing up. Brittany was a little bit tipsy. Several more strands of her piled-up hair had escaped and now curled wildly around her face. A bead of sweat rolled down between her collarbone, making its way straight for the vee in her dress between her luscious breasts.

He forced himself not to follow its progress.

"He probably doesn't really think so, either," she said, annoyed. "He was flattering me. That's what men do when they find a woman attractive."

She said this as if Mitch needed a few lessons in how to treat a woman, which he would be the first to admit he needed.

"I wasn't referring to the pink stripe in your hair," he informed her levelly. "You're not going home with him."

She looked at least as astonished as he felt that those words had come out of his mouth.

"When you're ready to go, I'll take you home," he said, his voice deliberately quiet.

"But I told Farley—"

"You came with me," he snapped. "It's my responsibility to see you safely home."

"Oh. Your *responsibility*."

"That's right."

She glared at him. "I'm not six and I already told Farley—"

"I don't give a damn what you told him."

"What are you going to do? You can't *make* me go with you instead of him."

"Yes, I can."

She narrowed her eyes at him. It occurred to him eyes like that, such a multitude of confusing colors, should be declared illegal.

"And how can you do that?" she asked defiantly. "Frankly, you don't seem like the type to make a scene."

"Frankly, you don't know the first thing about me," he told her quietly.

"I know you are not the type to toss a girl over your shoulder and storm out of the room like some Neanderthal fresh from the cave."

The picture that flashed through his mind was not at all unappealing. "Don't tempt me," he warned her.

"Mitch Hamilton, I am twenty-seven years old, and you are not going to tell me what to do."

"Why is it I have this feeling no one has ever succeeded in telling you what to do?"

"That's correct," she said with satisfaction.

Here's what she didn't know. He dealt with some of this community's toughest kids on a regular basis. He had a knack—a furrow of brow, a deepening of voice, a flex of muscle—that encouraged them to see things his way. Still, facing a drug-crazed kid with a knife had nothing on facing her, not that he was going to let that show.

"Maybe it's about time someone did," he said, his voice deliberately calm, level. "Your friend who wants to drive you home is forty-seven years old. He's been married three times. He brags about his conquests over morning coffee."

And if she became one of them, Mitch had the awful feeling he'd fly across the coffee table and have old Farley up against the wall, his shirt wrapped in his fists, in the blink of an eye.

A bit of the street fighter was still in him, the rebel, the bad boy was not completely banished as he had thought.

Farley was coming toward them now, and Mitch saw with some satisfaction her eyes were fastened on his own taut biceps, before they flickered, full of doubt, to Farley.

Mitch stepped in front of Brittany, folded his arms over his chest, and placed his feet astride. "She came with me. I'm going to take her home."

He waited for Brittany to leap from behind him and protest, and was amazed by her meek silence.

"She came with you? I had no idea," Farley said, all smooth charm, completely unruffled.

"He's got some old-fashioned notion that he needs to

take me home,'' Brittany said from behind Mitch. "But you can call me, Farley.''

She said Farley's name with enough sugar in it that she could have been trying out for the part of Scarlett at the ball.

Mitch saw Farley glance at his face, and knew he saw there what Mitch managed to keep hidden most of the time, a wild place that would never be quite tamed. Mitch knew, with a sensation of satisfaction he did not want to investigate, that Farley would not be calling Brittany anytime soon.

Mitch turned to her. "Let's go.''

"Humph,'' she said, tilting her nose in the air.

She stumbled on the stair out, and he took her elbow. Her skin was warm beneath his fingertips, and soft. He actually regretted that he had not overcome his pride and danced with her one more time.

He was not a man accustomed to regrets.

"Is it necessary for you to make me feel like a prisoner under escort?'' she asked.

He ignored her, and did not release her elbow. When they got to his car, he opened the passenger side door and shoved her inside. When he went around to the driver's side, she had her face turned out her window and she kept it that way.

They drove to her place in silence. He got out and went around to her door, which she allowed him to open for her, but she jerked away from his steadying hand this time, and went up the lane and the stairs to her door in front of him. He walked her to the door not because he was foolish enough to expect—or want—a repeat of that kiss, but because the alleyway did not look like a safe place for a woman at this time of night.

"Good night, Mitch,'' she said coolly at the top of her steps.

"Brittany," he returned, just as coolly. He waited to hear the bolt slide shut on her door before he walked away. He walked down the stairs, thinking, with relief and regret mingled in equal parts. *It's over.*

His obligation to Jordan was fulfilled.

"Mitch, it's coffee time."

Mitch glanced up at his office door. His adoptive father, Jordan, stood there. He debated telling him he couldn't go today.

But they went for coffee every morning together. Had been doing so since Mitch joined the firm six years ago.

Unfortunately, they usually went just down the street to the Main Street Bakery, and he had not forgotten Brittany telling him her grand reopening was today.

Mitch took his jacket off the back of his chair, stood up and shrugged into it. Using the mirror on the back of a closet door, he straightened his tie. His eyes had dark crescents under them.

"You look tired, Mitch. Is everything all right?" Jordan asked.

"Sure," he said.

But the truth was, it wasn't. He felt like he hadn't slept a wink since Saturday night. Haunted by the taste of her lips, the fire in her eyes, the toss of her head. Haunted by his own behavior.

The last thing he needed to do was go to her bakery and see how she was blundering along, her idealistic dreams on an inevitable collision course with cold, hard reality.

And he doubted if he could make himself stay away. He'd been tempted to drop in all morning. It was an unsettling feeling for a man as accustomed to control as he was, to be so tempted, to feel so pulled to the very thing that most threatened his control.

"Did you enjoy yourself Saturday night?" Jordan asked him, as they strolled down the street.

Mitch slid him a look. "It was okay," he said noncommittally.

"Those triplets are beautiful, every one of them, but Brittany seems to have an extra—" He paused looking for words.

"Spark?" Mitch suggested drily.

"That's it! She seems on fire with life."

"Whatever."

"You didn't like her?" Jordan asked. "She seems like such a nice girl."

"Dad, you aren't matchmaking are you?"

"Of course not." This said too quickly.

"Because it would be beneath you. I think Mrs. Pondergrove is a bad influence on you. That's the type of thing I can see her doing."

"Angela only wants people to be happy."

"I'm happy just the way I am. You can pass that on to Angela, if you happen to see her."

"Mitch, to be frank, you don't seem to have much of a life. Work. Those kids at the community center where you volunteer. A man needs more than that."

"Well, not this man."

"Monica made you bitter," Jordan decided.

Being jilted at the altar had a tendency to do that. Mitch said nothing.

"Why don't you just get to know the Patterson girl a bit? What would it hurt?"

"She's looking—with a frightening single-minded purpose—for something quite different than me."

"Happiness?" Jordan suggested.

"Marriage!" he replied, as if this answer should have been obvious to his father.

"She's a lonely kid in a strange town taking on a whole new set of circumstances. She'll need a friend."

"Fine, send old Angela over to visit her."

"I don't like it when you refer to Angela in that tone of voice. She's a good woman with a kind heart."

"Sorry, Dad." A good woman with a kind heart, *and* a meddlesome way.

"Would you look at that?" Jordan said with amazement as they approached the bakery. "Is that a lineup?"

It was a lineup, going right outside the door, and curving in front of the newly lettered front window. Heavenly Treats.

"It's good to see her doing so well," Jordan said.

But Mitch, not blessed with the same spirit of undaunted optimism as his father, quickly realized the line wasn't moving forward. Several people left in disgust. He suspected, not that she was doing well, but that she wasn't coping with even the normal crowd.

"Let's go somewhere else," Mitch said.

"Slip in there and see what's going on," Jordan said. "Maybe you can help her out."

Mitch shot his father a look that Jordan ignored.

"How could I help her out? I don't know anything about bakeries."

"Neither does she."

Mitch saw the set of his father's chin, and drew in a deep breath. There were some occasions when you didn't argue with Jordan Hamilton.

"Excuse me," he said. Drawing in a deep breath, he shoved his way through the little bottleneck in the doorway, ignoring the irritated looks he got.

Inside, the smell of fresh paint overpowered the smell of baking.

The paint job was probably the worst he'd ever seen. The wallpaper was on crooked, the patterns unmatched.

Black and white posters of Humphrey Bogart, Marilyn Monroe and James Dean had been hung at random, he suspected over the worst of the paint job. He thought she'd achieved a kind of wartime café ambience, as if everything was a little shaken because of the last bombing, but they were bravely open for business anyway. He somehow doubted that was the atmosphere she'd been aiming for.

The few little tables were already covered with dishes that had not been cleared away.

The brand-new tablecloths, pink with an overlay of lace, had coffee stains and crumbs on them. The fresh flowers, stems of daisies, drooped.

The customers were cranky.

And there she was, behind her counter, a white apron, with spilt coffee on it over a dress that looked like it was meant to be worn at a summer church picnic—on second glance, he realized it might be just a touch too sexy for the church picnic—her hair falling out of its neat ponytail, her mascara smudged, a look of determined cheer on her face that was faltering.

"What do you mean you're out of doughnuts?" the man was blustering at her. "I've had a doughnut in here every day for fifteen years."

Mitch glanced at her display cases. On the shelf that usually overflowed with honey-glazed and chocolate and sugar doughnuts, were lacy little pastries and several large, round chocolate cakes. Not a single slice was missing from the cakes. Hand lettered signs, an awful imitation of calligraphy, announced the cakes were Chocolate Mocha Torte and Carmel Fudge Delight.

"We're branching off from doughnuts," she told the man with determined pluck. "Wouldn't you like to try some chocolate mocha torte?"

"No," the man snapped at her. "I wouldn't. Just give me a coffee."

"Irish Cream Cappuccino or French Vanilla?" she asked.

Leave, Mitch ordered himself. He'd seen enough and there was nothing he could do. Not that he was sure his father would see things quite the same way. Damn. From the very beginning Jordan had forced him to be a better person than Mitch believed he really was.

"I just want a blasted cup of good old American coffee, the same as I've had every morning for fifteen years," the customer said loudly. "Is that too much to ask?"

Mitch made the mistake of glancing back at her. Her face seemed so pale. The smile finally broke, and if he was not mistaken her bottom lip, full and dewy, was trembling.

And the paint was still in her hair.

With a sigh, he pushed through the throng to the front.

For a moment, he thought he saw relief in her eyes. And then she pulled herself to her full height of about five feet five inches, and said, "I'm sorry, sir, you'll have to wait in line like everyone else."

The thing about doing the decent thing was that not everyone appreciated it.

He leaned toward her. "Cut up one of those chocolate things into little bite-size pieces, and put it on a plate. Don't even think of arguing with me."

She opened her mouth, obviously thinking of arguing with him, glanced at the man who was still steaming about his American coffee, and then, with ill grace whirled away and got her largest cake out of the display.

Wielding the knife with a little more temper than might have been absolutely necessary she chopped a section of the cake into chunks for him, and shoved it at him.

"Chocolate mocha *torte,*" she said firmly. "Is that all, sir?"

He took the plate from her, shook his head at her miffed kitten expression, and smiled at the lady who was next in line—the bank teller from First Oregon—who was glancing at her watch and obviously fuming.

"Would you like to try some of this?" he said. "Chocolate mocha *torte*. Don't be fooled. It looks just like cake, but it isn't. One of the house specialties. And how about you, Mr. Smith? How's business at the hardware store today?"

He made his way down the line, chatting with friends and neighbors and business associates. They were happier once they were eating, especially since it was free.

Out of the corner of his eye, he saw his dad slip in the door and start clearing tables. That was his dad. One of the most prosperous and respected men in this town, and yet he retained an air of complete humility, a desire to truly be of service to his fellow man, that left Mitch in awe of him.

Jordan Hamilton was quite simply his hero.

Mitch would go to the ends of the earth for him if he was asked.

"Mitch, go behind the counter and give her a hand for a few minutes."

Why did that seem like a larger request than going to the ends of the earth? He wanted to point out to his dad that it was a temporary solution to a permanent problem. The girl was in over her head. He couldn't come and help her out every day.

Still, he gave the plate of torte to a customer in the line. "Take one and pass it on."

He went and flipped up the counter, and ducked under it. He took off his jacket and rolled up his sleeves. Instead of looking grateful, she gave him a dirty look, which he ignored.

Out of the corner of his eye, he took a closer look at the dress, hidden behind the apron.

A sundress. If he was not mistaken that slit that began at the neckline went all the way to her navel. He was suddenly glad she had the apron on. The dress would be perfect for a yacht party with Brad Pitt, but was hopelessly inappropriate for a counter girl at a bakery.

Suspiciously, he looked at her feet and saw stiletto heels, with narrow little straps holding them on around her slender ankles. She already was shifting uncomfortably from one foot to the other.

"I can manage," she hissed, then saw where he was looking. She planted both daintily shod feet firmly on the floor, but he didn't miss the wince.

"Who's next here?" he asked.

He took good-natured ribbing from people he knew, listened to complaints, soothed ruffled feathers, poured coffee, promised doughnuts tomorrow and gave away free pieces of torte to the people who were really mad.

The rush died.

"Mr. Hamilton, don't do that!" Brittany ducked under the counter and retrieved a mess of dishes on a tray from his father. "You're embarrassing me."

"Embarrassing you?" his father said. "Why at my age it's a privilege to play knight to a lady in need."

Mitch contemplated his father's chivalry with an emotion he recognized with annoyance might be envy.

She came back around the counter loaded with too many dishes. "You didn't get any of your father's charm, did you?" she whispered to him.

He took the tray from her. "I'm adopted."

He saw just a moment's hesitation, as if she wanted to cling to that common ground between them as if it were a life raft. The moment passed. "That would explain it. Back there."

He took the tray and guided it safely through a swinging door that led to the kitchen and set it down on the only clean spot on the counter. The sinks were both stacked to overflowing. She came in behind him.

He wasn't sure how, but she smelled sweet. A lemony smell that reminded him of spring and sunshine.

He watched her face as she looked at the dishes, saw the slump to her shoulders.

"Thanks, Mitch," she said stiffly. "Not that I don't appreciate the help, but I really think I could have managed."

He refrained from asking for her definition of managing.

"It's my first day, after all." She put one hand on the wall, leaned sideways and lifted a foot. She took off the flimsy sandal and massaged. "Abby offered to come help, but even I couldn't ask my sister to spend her honeymoon like this."

Something in her changed every time she talked about her sisters. The fiery light in her mellowed, glowed softer. He was unhappy that he noticed that.

"And your other sister?"

"She had to go back to Minnesota right away. She's not moving here for a few more weeks." She looked at him shrewdly, and then as if guessing he might be able to see some softness in her, she turned on her megawatt smile. "Do you think you might want to marry her?"

"I'm not the marrying kind."

Did she look relieved that he had refused her sister just as readily as he had refused her? He couldn't tell. Her hair, by accident or design, swung over her face and her toes suddenly commanded all her attention.

"I don't think those shoes are, er, suitable for this kind of work. You might want to think of those shoes like the nurses wear. Flat-soled. Orthopedic."

"Flat-soled orthopedic shoes," she repeated, then sighed. "That would probably go quite nicely with my pink hair. Not to mention this apron. It's ghastly."

"It's not a fashion show, Brittany," he said, amazed by the gentleness in his tone.

"Oh, like I didn't figure that out ten minutes after the

door opened. Okay," she said, dismissively. "I'm fine," she insisted, holding open the swinging door for him to walk through. "Take a piece of torte on the house. Good-bye."

He shrugged into his jacket, as she disappeared through the door again. He'd almost made it around the counter, when he heard it.

Muffled. Soft. Like a little hiccup.

Leave, he told himself, but he leaned a little closer to the door, listened a little harder. Damn.

No doubt about it. She was back there crying.

"Dad, you go ahead. I'll be along in a minute."

His dad looked inordinately pleased about that.

He went back through the swinging door into the kitchen. She was sitting on a little stool that looked like a milking stool, her shoes off, her head buried in her hands and her shoulders shaking. As he watched, she took a corner of her white apron and dabbed at her eyes with it.

"Hey," he said softly, "it really will be okay, you know." He said that with as much conviction as he could muster in the face of the fact he was not at all certain it was true.

There. How was that for chivalrous?

Apparently terrible.

Because she leapt to her feet, wiped at her eyes again with the back of her hand, and leveled him a look of proud disdain.

"How dare you spy on me!"

"I wasn't spying. I heard you—"

"I don't need your help! I can do it by myself."

"Oh, I saw that." A truly chivalrous man would have said something else.

"You caught me at a bad moment."

"I'll say." For all the years of school and law, the rogue

still spoke first—blunt, cutting, lacking totally in gifts of diplomacy.

"It was not as bad as it looked."

"That's good, because it looked plenty bad." He sighed at the mutinous expression on her face, and tried to wrestle the rebel back behind his wall of refinement. He used a different tone.

"Have you considered hiring someone? Just for the rush periods? I know some kids who might—"

"Don't you understand, Mitch Hamilton?" she said bravely, though her lip was trembling, again, and it filled him with the desire to go and cover her mouth with his own. "I don't want your help. I wouldn't accept help from you if... if you were the last man on earth!"

Nothing less than he deserved, he thought.

What he didn't quite understand was why, when it should have felt like a reprieve, it felt like she had put an arrow through his left arm. A long way from the heart, thank God.

"Fine," he said, turning on his heel. "Bungle through on your own. I don't give a damn."

"That's fine with me. I'll invite you to the awards ceremony when Heavenly Treats is named Business-of-the-Year."

"I'll send my tux to the cleaners and have a snack or two between now and then," he said, his parting shot. Then he wondered, as he walked back to his office, if anyone had ever gotten under his skin quite the way she did.

No one ever had.

Ever.

And he was not quite sure what that meant, but he was pretty sure it wasn't good.

Chapter Three

The phone rang. Brittany opened one eye, regarded the phone, and then her feet, which she was soaking in a rubber tub of hot water. Answering the phone would mean either wiping her feet off, or dribbling water across the floor to the phone.

Water *she* would have to wipe up.

All those years of dribbling water wherever she wanted after a shower or a long soak, and never once giving a thought about who wiped up behind her.

The phone rang again, and she ignored it, putting her head against the wingback of her chair and groaning. It was seven o'clock at night and she was in her pajamas.

Oddly, thinking about who had picked up and cleaned up behind her didn't make her feel wistful for her old life. It made her feel slightly guilty. Little apple-cheeked Anya, scurrying around quietly, always smiling, nodding her head, "Yes ma'am. Yes ma'am."

It wasn't that she'd ever been unkind to the staff of her parents' house. It wasn't that at all. She had just never treated them like people worthy of her liking and respect. She had treated them more like the furniture.

Brittany had been in the real world for five days now, having people treat her like the furniture, her position to unobtrusively serve them.

"I said *chocolate* doughnuts."

"What do you mean you don't have multigrain today? You always have multigrain!"

"I've been waiting seven minutes for service."

"I gave you a ten, not a five."

"I won't take this birthday cake. You spelled Tonya with a *j*."

Really, she had no talent for being unobtrusive. But even the bright colors, and the wonderful flare of Angela Missoni and Ralph Lauren casual clothing—perfect for work—could not pick up her flagging spirits. She had given up her lovely shoes, and was now wearing orthopedic nursing shoes. Her feet still hurt, just not as badly.

Her friends in California would kill themselves laughing at those shoes, and at the picture of her in her pajamas soaking her feet in a dingy apartment at seven o'clock at night.

California. A little warmer than here at this stage of April. Once upon a time, she would have been shopping for bikinis.

And friends? The calls had dried up at about the same time as the money. She told herself it was okay. They had never really known her, anyway. Not the real her. They'd known the girl who partied and wore the latest and drove the best.

Frankly, even Brit was a little astonished to be finding out how little those things had to do with *her,* even if she would have loved to have them back. She regarded them almost like a security blanket she had outgrown.

Could she go back now? If she won a million dollars,

would she ever be the girl she had been six months ago? She disliked even thinking such complicated thoughts, and knew in a way she could not quite fathom, this self-analysis had something to do with *him.*

The phone rang again, and she sighed and wiped a tear from her cheek. What was it about this stupid town that had her in tears all the time? The truth was she was exhausted and more than a little scared.

This was her first real job, and she hated it. She had thought it would be easy and fun to run a business and nothing could be further from the truth. The "funnest" part of her day was turning the sign on the front door from Open to Closed.

The brutal truth was she was failing. Miserably. She couldn't even sell bread, for God's sake. She was terrible at making change, not fast enough, and not even as cheerful and upbeat as she had planned to be. By the end of the day, her soul and feet aching, her wonderful clothes drenched in sweat and flour and coffee, she was snarling at her customers. "What do you want?"

The tortes were a complete bomb, and Luigi, the baker, was grumbling ominously about the specialty pastries. He was also upset that she had spent money on painting and new tablecloths when he said the exposed water pipe that ran through the kitchen dripped on his head at unexpected moments, something she had yet to witness.

Despite his unpleasant personality, it was a good thing Luigi made the best bread and doughnuts and baked treats she had ever sampled. People kept coming, putting up with her ineptness to get to his baking.

Only maybe they weren't going to have to tolerate her ineptness much longer. There had to be a way out of this mess, and she stayed awake at nights thinking over different possibilities. Now she had several in mind, and she rehearsed pitching them to Mitch until she had the nerve to talk to him. His secretary said he would call back, probably tomorrow since she had reached his office right at five.

She heard her voice on the answering machine, perky and upbeat, the person she used to be.

"Hi, you've reached me, and you know the drill. I'll get back to you."

How could she have been so stupid as to put that ad in the paper right now? Husband Wanted. Every weirdo within a thousand-mile radius was calling her. Why hadn't she thought of a post office box? Now, she was probably going to have to change her phone number. She already had to unplug it at night so she could sleep.

She had to face it. The reasons she had put that ad in the paper didn't have that much to do with the amount of time she had invested in painting. Some of the reasons had been because of *him*. To deny the feelings he stirred in her. To dismiss them. To take her power back. To say feelings are feelings, but marriage is business.

She thought of him seeing the ad, the dark cloud of disapproval that would cross his face, turn down his lips, when he read it. He would have to know it was her. Have to.

"Hi, Brit, it's Abby. I feel like I've called in all my favors, but could I get one more teensy one? Will you help me fit the dress I'm making for Mrs. Pondergrove? Sunday morning would be good. Around eleven. Call me back."

Brittany sighed. She wished Corrine was here to help take on some of these sisterly duties.

Still, couldn't Mrs. Pondergrove try on her own dress? Then, vaguely she remembered the old lady was having a wedding gown made for someone.

Really, the last thing Brittany wanted to be doing was trying on wedding dresses. She had helped Abby with the fittings for the dress Abby had eventually gotten married in. A beautiful dress that had felt so foreign, and so *wrong* on Brittany.

It was probably an omen. No wedding in her future. Which meant no bakery. And no job. Now *that* made her feel wistful, even if she didn't have a clue what she would do with her life if her bakery disappeared.

"I'd think of something," she muttered, scowling as she inspected the fingernail she had broken in the bread-slicing machine. Her hands didn't even look like her hands. The fingernails were unvarnished, and cut absurdly short.

The phone rang again.

"Shut up," she begged it. And after a few rings it did as the answering machine clicked on.

"Hey, babe, if you're looking for a guy to hitch with, I'm your cowboy. I've left six messages and you ain't answered yet. I'm getting impatient to get my rope on you, you little filly. I'll bet you're screening your calls, so honey, I'm gonna hang up and call you right back."

"Death sounds good," she said to the ceiling. All she had wanted was a husband, tall, dark and handsome—

The phone rang again. She removed her feet from the water, which was growing cold anyway, and stomped across the floor, heedless of the puddles.

She picked up the receiver and said, "I'm not your little filly, and if you ever call here again, the only rope you'll feel is the one I'll be putting around your neck."

Silence.

Suddenly, she *knew* who it was, and it wasn't any cowboy trying to rope a filly. It was Mitch Hamilton, who by some mysterious working of kismet was always the first one on the scene whenever her mind entertained foolish notions about husbands.

She should be cured by now.

"Brittany?"

She sighed. "Mitch."

"Returning your call."

"Thank you for calling after hours." She had told him

he was the last man on earth she would ever turn to for help, but the truth was, she needed help.

A loophole. Someway he could get her out of that bakery. She needed to know if she leased it to Luigi if she would still be fulfilling the conditions of her gift.

"What's going on? Are you getting phone calls you don't want to get?"

"You might say that." Why, why, *why* did he have to be the one to catch her in these awful moments? She'd been expecting his call all evening, rehearsing what she would say, planning to impress him with her composure and cultivation.

"Obscene calls?" he asked.

She pondered the genuine worry in his voice. "More like nuisance calls."

"Call the police." His voice was stern. He was giving her an order! Again. He was easily the most bossy, controlling man she had ever met.

She might have been miffed by his heavy-handedness, except the concern was still there, adding the strangest timbre to his sexy voice, making a shiver go up and down her spine, reminding her of the taste of his lips on hers, the feel of his hand on her naked back, the smoldering look in his blue eyes.

Besides, she needed a favor.

"I kind of brought the calls on myself," she admitted reluctantly.

"How?"

"Um, I put an ad in the paper."

"What kind of ad. For your bakery?"

"Uh, not exactly."

"Lawyers kind of like the *exactly* part."

"Exactly?" she stalled.

He was silent, but she could almost hear his lawyer's

brain sorting information, calculating, deducing. He actually swore.

"I didn't think you knew that word," she said, feigning shock.

"I told you I have a dark past. You put the ad in the paper for a husband, didn't you?"

"Uh, well—"

"This is a yes or no question."

"Being a witness in a case you were involved in wouldn't be a particularly pleasant experience, would it?"

"Answer the damned question. Did you put an ad in the paper that you were looking for a husband?"

"Yes," she said, without a trace of the remorse she was feeling, "I did." She could picture what he looked like right now, dark brows arrowing down over his eyes, mouth taut, eyes narrowed. Just the reaction she had imagined him having when he read her ad.

Which he hadn't. She'd been fielding all these horrible calls for nothing.

He was silent for a long time, and then he said, his voice calm, "You put your phone number in the ad?"

"It's all your fault, Mitch. You said no. Just think, you and I could have been Mr. and Mrs. Hamilton by now." She was quite pleased with the way that came out. Light. Teasing. As if her soul had not been bruised black-and-blue by his rejection of her rather slurred proposal.

A very reasonable rejection, if she wanted to be fair about it. She didn't.

"Do you ever just out-and-out answer a question? You'd be my worst nightmare on a witness stand."

"Really?" she said, feeling a little sliver of pleasure. At least she was in his dreams.

"So, you put your phone number in the paper. Something wrong with a box number?"

"Please don't tell me how stupid that was. Believe me, I've already figured that out."

He sighed, audibly, and again she could picture him. Rolling his shoulders, trying to shrug off his impatience with her. She wondered what he was wearing. She glanced at the clock. He'd be home from the office, probably. Did he dress down, now? Jeans and a sweatshirt?

Maybe he was in his underwear.

"So, have you at least canceled the ad?" he asked.

She gasped theatrically.

He swore again.

And then she laughed. "Of course I've canceled the ad. Until I rethink the wording. And get a box number."

"You're determined to go through with this?"

"Hey, I need a husband. Anybody will do."

But just hearing his voice, strong and steady, on the other end of the line, she knew she was not going to be satisfied with just anybody anymore.

"If I end up marrying you to save you from yourself, I'm going to be damned unhappy about it," he said.

It occurred to her this was a step up from *not if you were the last woman on earth* though not even she could be flattered at him being damned unhappy about the prospect of marrying her.

"Did you call for a reason?" she snapped.

"I'm returning *your* call."

"Oh. Right. I need to meet with you. It's urgent."

"Legal business?"

"You might say that."

"The exact answer, again. Hang on. I'll check my calendar. I can squeeze you in tomorrow, at eleven."

"I can't get away from the bakery. I hate to ask you to give up part of your weekend, but it shouldn't take long, and—"

"Sunday, at eleven-thirty?"

"Perfect. I'm going to be at my sister's. Could you meet me there?" She gave him the address.

He didn't say a word about giving up his weekend, or making house calls. Or what he charged, and she had been afraid to ask him. The bakery revenues were down since her takeover. This week she was going to be able to pay Luigi and buy a few cans of tuna. She'd splurge on a head of lettuce. At least she had all the bread she could ever eat.

"See you Sunday," he said, curtly, no kiss haunting him, apparently.

She sighed, unplugged her phone, and went and put her feet back in the water.

Mitch put down the phone and stared at it for a moment, and then looked at the clock. Nearly eight. Too late to be in the office. What paper would that ad have been in, before she canceled it?

He went out the door, and started. His secretary, a big woman who wore sweaters even in the summer and had the kindest face he'd ever seen, was still there.

"Hey," he said guiltily, "go home to your kids."

"Oh, my boys are in golf now, and Henry's out of town. I don't have anything better to do. Did you need something?"

"Copies of last week's newspapers?" he said hopefully.

"The *Miracle Harbor Beacon?*"

He nodded.

She laughed. "You never read that paper. It has the bridge scores in it!"

"So?" he said. "Maybe I want to know who won."

"Sally and Hiram Wilson," she called his bluff. "Actually, I think there might be a few days' worth in the coffee room."

"Thanks, Millie."

He went down to the coffee room, and saw the office

was having a pool. A paper was divided into squares each labeled with possible birth dates for one of the secretaries who was hugely pregnant. Farley had purchased nearly every available box, as always. Mitch hadn't been invited to join. Maybe Brittany Patterson saw him as stiff and uptight because that was what he was.

He found a stack of old newspapers, glanced at the door, and then fingers flying, he found the want ads. Personals.

Good God. She had done it. There it was, in big black letters. Husband Wanted. He read on. Must be gainfully employed or well-established financially. A sense of humor essential—

He felt the disapproving crease in his forehead and deliberately tried to erase it.

—between ages thirty and fifty-five—

Fifty-five? What the hell was she thinking? That an old man could make her happy? An old man would be worn out by all that energy in about thirty seconds. With the exception of Farley Houser, of course. He rubbed at the reappearing crease.

—enjoy traveling, theater, candlelight dinners, bubble baths for two—

Well, that would explain the weirdos calling her! Bubble baths for two. His rebel put in a sudden appearance and wagged his eyebrows fiendishly.

—and must be totally fearless in the face of insects of all varieties, and particularly spiders.

Mitch didn't want to laugh. He really didn't. It had been very foolish of her to place this ad in a public paper, making herself vulnerable. Still, a rusty chuckle crept by his guard, and then another.

He realized he hadn't laughed for a long time. What was there in his life to laugh about?

He read the part about spiders again and laughed some

more. She had concluded with, P.S. Good looks helpful, but not essential.

He found that funny, too.

His secretary popped her head in the coffee room door and looked at him quizzically.

"Maybe I should get a subscription after all," he said. He closed the paper before she could see what section he was in.

She smiled at him. "I'm going for the day. And Mr. Hamilton?"

"Yes?"

"It's really good to see you laugh." She closed the door behind herself.

He sat for a moment pondering that. Was Brittany right? Had he become far too serious? Become? he chided himself. He had always been serious.

He'd been born that way.

His earliest memories were of trying to hold things together. A little boy looking after his brothers, struggling with the weight of his baby sister. Trying so hard to keep them safe and clean, trying to keep food in the house. He remembered, suddenly, stealing bread from a corner store. It was only now, looking back, he realized the owner had probably let him take it.

His whole young life had been about trying to keep his mom sober. If only he could be more perfect maybe she wouldn't drink.

He took a deep breath. A man thought he left things behind him, but he didn't really. They became a part of him. Those paperclips lined up in a neat row on his desk, everything in his life so ordered and perfect. All linking back to his aversion to the chaos of his past, and to his even deeper thinking that if he could be perfect enough he could fix the whole world.

The days of his growing up had left marks on him Jordan

Hamilton could not repair. He liked being in control. He didn't let go easily, or know a great deal about having fun.

This introspection shocked him, and somehow he knew it was about her, shaking up his neat and tidy world, knocking stuff to the surface that he had held down, deliberately, for a long, long time.

But maybe it was never too late to learn a different way.

And his rebel was more than happy to tell him who could teach him all about having fun. Bubble baths for two. He'd never even had a bubble bath for one.

And he knew, now, it was going to be impossible to be satisfied with that.

"Ouch! Abby!"

"Sorry. Brit, can't you stand still?"

"Not one of my specialties. This dress is very different than yours was, isn't it?" Shane had taken Belle, who wanted to touch the fabric, into the kitchen. Now Brit could hear the low rumble of his laughter and Belle's squeals of delight. This house seemed full to the brim with love and laughter.

"About as different as night and day," Abby said. "You know, Mrs. Pondergrove still won't tell me who it's for."

Brit really didn't care about the intrigues of old Mrs. Pondergrove's life. Brit could not give herself over to the easy joy of Shane and Abby's house, much as she wanted to. She felt nervous as a cat—but not because she was going to see Mitch again.

Well, maybe that, too.

But what was she going to say to him? Could she admit defeat without letting on how defeated she was?

"She's having this dress made to replace the one she gave to me," Abby went on. "She said it's for someone to whom she owes a great debt."

"Well, that's weird," Brit said absently. Soon she would

be putting back on the outfit she'd worn over here, an off-the-rack canary-yellow pop top and matching Capri pants. The ensemble was darling and showed enough belly button and leg that he might be off balance. Might not even hear the underlying desperation when she told him she had become bored with the bakery, felt she was unsuited for it, wanted to trade it in for something a little more glamorous.

"I'm going to give Mrs. Pondergrove this dress for free," Abby decided.

For a girl who had been eating tuna salad all week the idea of Abby giving her services away was preposterous. "For free?" Brit wailed. "Don't do that!"

"I have to. I have this little voice inside telling me what to do."

"How come I don't have a little voice that tells me what to do?"

Abby laughed, and Brit loved the sound of her sister laughing, and thought even if nothing else was going exactly the way she'd imagined it, having a sister was better than she had dreamed it could be.

"Of course you have a little voice that tells you what to do. Everyone does. Intuition. Spirit. Whatever you want to call it, you have it. You just don't listen."

"Well, it should have told me not to put that ad in the paper. The creeps have finally stopped phoning. Look, could you hurry? I told Mitch to meet me here—"

"Mitch?" Abby breathed.

"Forget it. He's not interested. I gave him first chance, and he gave me first refusal." Brit thought she had long ago perfected that light, laughter-filled voice that hid how she really felt, so she was surprised when Abby did not even look a little bit convinced.

"Well, if he's not interested, why's he meeting you here?"

"Oh, I need a little legal advice about something, and

you know how it is when you operate your own business. It's tough to get away.'' She didn't say if she closed for an hour to keep an appointment, she might be eating beans next week.

"Is everything going all right with the bakery? It looked hectic when I came in last week.''

Hectic was so much nicer than chaotic. Brit loved Abby's effortless diplomacy. "It's going fabulously,'' she said.

Abby gave her a worried look. "I can come help, you know.''

Brittany felt ashamed. Her sister, with a baby, and a sewing business of her own, and a brand-new husband, offering to help her.

"I said it was going fabulously,'' she said, a touch tersely.

"It's nice of Mitch to see you on the weekend.''

"I bet he's a workaholic.''

"I bet he wants to see you. I saw him kiss you at the wedding.''

"Oh. That. Too much champagne.'' She decided to leave out the part about the too much champagne being strictly on her side.

"I'm done. Have a look before you take it off.''

Brittany swung around, and looked in her sister's full-length mirror. The breath caught in her chest, and her heart began to beat with a rapid thud that she could hear in her own ears.

The dress was absolutely gorgeous, something out of a dream. Or a fairy tale. It was formfitting and low-cut over the bodice, thin straps holding it at the shoulders. The material, a sexy shiny film of satin, clung around the slenderness of her hips and thighs and then flared gloriously at the knee. There was the faintest pattern of gold roses in the material.

"The bodice will have gold-beaded roses on it," Abby said dreamily. "And I have to make a wrap to go with it. Oh, hon, that dress was made for you."

"It's not like any wedding dress I've ever seen before," Brittany stammered. The dress, despite the shimmering white of the fabric, was not innocent in the least, but electric. It celebrated the curves and softness of a woman. It taunted and beguiled and whispered.

And it made Brittany think the oddest thoughts. Not of marrying for necessity, or for personal gain, but of marrying for love.

To have a romance—a wonderful romp through the regions of her heart, to live for the sound of another person's voice, the look in his eyes, the touch of his hands.

To live with a certain lightness of soul, to celebrate the wonders of life, to dance with laughter every day.

Her eyes were filming over again, as she contemplated what real weddings, the kind where a woman wore a dress like this, were about. Not convenience. Not security. Not material gain.

A dress like this was about the dream of a man looking at you a certain way. A man *wanting* to walk all the days of his life, with his hand in yours, a man who wanted to say the word husband when he gazed at you, and wanted it to mean forever.

A tear slipped out, and ran down her cheek to the corner of her mouth. She tasted the salt in it. Someone to love her. Was that so much to ask for?

She wiped at the tear, but when she looked up the mist remained over her eyes. And when she looked back in the mirror, she gasped.

For in the reflection, he stood behind her, looking at her, some unguarded passion turning his eyes a darker shade of blue, a shade that held all the mysteries of sea and sky, universe and earth, man and woman.

For an eerie moment, she felt almost as if reality had shifted, as if the dress had created its own reality, and that him standing there, hands deep in jean pockets, shoulder braced against her sister's doorway, was only part of the delicious illusion that she had been immersed in since the moment she had felt the coolness of the fabric against her naked flesh.

But then, she realized it was really him.

Catching her in another moment of pure vulnerability. She didn't have that many! Why was he always in the right place at the wrong time?

And why was he always in the picture whenever she entertained the notion of becoming Mrs. Somebody?

"Ordering the dress?" he said sardonically. "I thought you hadn't sifted through all your applications for grooms yet."

She sniffed and tilted her chin high. "There's no sense being caught unprepared."

"Now that," he said, and smiled, "sounds like something I would say."

And it was his smile that made Brittany yearn for the picture she had glimpsed so briefly in the mirror, of herself and him, to be real.

Chapter Four

Mitch stared at Brittany, feeling like he'd taken a wrong turn somewhere and ended up smack-dab in the middle of a fairy tale.

A place that a lawyer, a man renowned for his pragmatism, his ability to think clearly and with clarity, certainly didn't want to be.

He wondered how he knew it was Brittany in the swirling dress that seemed to be made of mist and silk, and not her sister. He knew somehow it was something more than the fact that he couldn't picture Brit on the floor with her mouth full of pins.

The two women were identical.

But what had his father said about Brittany? Fire.

Brittany was on fire, and that dress threatened to ignite everything around her, starting with Mitch Hamilton. He wanted to think he didn't know what kind of dress it was, that it might be a ball gown, or the world's sexiest negligee.

But he knew he couldn't kid himself. It was a bridal gown.

It was just not like any bridal gown that he had ever seen before, not that he considered himself any kind of expert. The dress seemed too daring to be for a blushing bride. Too bold. Too sensual. Too Brittany. Except the look on her face was not sensual or bold. Her face was filled with a most delicate kind of wonder, a dreaminess, a longing to believe in all the things that gown stood for.

Romance. Love. Forever.

Not one of which Mitch Hamilton believed in himself.

He had once. It seemed like a long time ago. He'd been on top of the world, working for his father's law firm, just beginning to work as a mentor at the Miracle Harbor Teen Center, engaged to be married to a beautiful, intelligent woman who came from a world he had once thought he would never enter.

And then a single choice and it had been over.

A law firm in Portland wanted him. Offered him the package—the money, the prestige, the career with the explosive opportunities.

He'd wanted what he had in Miracle Harbor more. His father was getting older, those kids *needed* him.

Monica had been disgusted with his choice. With a wedding two weeks away—their wedding—she'd given him the ultimatum. Move up in the world or it was off.

It was off.

He wasn't sure if you could move any further up in the world than working with kids who needed help as badly as these ones at the teen center did.

She disagreed.

It was a point that was nonnegotiable.

Now, looking at Brittany in her wedding dress, he felt a certain degree of discomfort. Not quite a pain, but certainly discomfort.

Some man was going to be waiting for her, at an altar, as she glided down the aisle in that dress. Some man was going to see the light in her face, and know it was directed at him.

Soon.

And Mitch had said it wasn't going to be him.

He felt deeply the loss of that, felt, for the most fleeting moment, a desire to believe. To believe in fairy tales and happy endings, even for guys like him who had known more than their fair share of gritty realism.

Her eyes, in the mirror, dewy, found him. They looked more blue today, like pansies drooping in the midday heat. He supposed she would know how to do that with makeup.

"Ordering the dress?" he heard himself saying, forced the sardonic, uncaring edge into his voice.

He saw her chin lift, saw how quickly she reacted to protect herself from his arrow. "There's no sense being caught unprepared."

Despite the tilted chin and the spirited flash in her eyes, he saw the vulnerability that lurked just below the surface, and reined in his desire to build a big wall around himself so that she couldn't touch him. With her beauty. And idealism. And dreams.

He found himself, instead, lowering his defenses. The rebel in him was smiling, encouraging her to dream, telling him a dream or two never hurt anyone.

And when she smiled back, he knew even the rebel was shocked by how totally a man could be disarmed by the power that dreams held within them.

"It's not really my dress," she told him. "Abby's making it for someone. That little old lady who was with your dad at the wedding."

He considered that for a moment. Why on earth would Miss Meddle of Miracle Harbor, Angela Pondergrove, be having a dress like that made? He also considered the fact that he could not deny he felt disappointed in some way that the dress was not for Brittany.

Disappointed and relieved at the same time.

His lawyer's mind told him to feel those things simultaneously was impossible.

His rebel told him to get used to it.

"I'm a little early," he said. "Shane let me in. But I can wait outside until you're finished." What a good idea. Wait outside, where this particular dream wasn't.

"We're done," Abby told him, straightening and smiling at him. Her smile was sweet and soft, with none of the devil-may-care edge to it that her sister had. "Brit's just going to go get changed. Have a seat on the couch." The two women left the room.

He took a seat, feeling like a gauche boy picking up his date for the prom. As if he'd ever gone to the prom. He'd scorned the finer traditions, when really deep inside, he'd been afraid of his rough edges, afraid he would never fit in, afraid he would be exposed as an imposter, not really Jordan Hamilton's son, but a boy from the wrong side of the tracks.

What was it about Brittany Patterson that brought insecurities, that Mitch could have sworn had long been laid to rest, racing to the surface? What was it about her that erased university honors and six years of law practice, and made him feel like that angry kid who had hungered for things he never thought he could have?

Brittany reappeared in a moment, in hip-hugging pants, canary-yellow, that ended just below her knees, and a matching canary-yellow top that ended just above her belly button. She had the cutest belly button, and there was really no reason on earth he should resent her for showing it off, but he did. Over the whole ensemble, she had draped a too-large shirt.

"I know," she said, with a sigh. "The shirt is a disaster."

He didn't have a clue what she was talking about.

"I grabbed it off the back of the bathroom door," she confided sadly. "The pants ripped. That will teach me to buy off-the-rack."

It was unfair to a man to know that. That right underneath that huge shirt, those pants were ripped. If he angled properly he could probably catch a glimpse of what color of panties she wore, but not without looking like a total pervert. It really was totally unfair.

She seemed to think so, too. "Is it possible to sue Mini-Mart for selling poor quality merchandise? For damages? For placing me in this embarrassing predicament?"

"Mini-Mart suits are not my specialty," he told her.

"What is your specialty?"

"Next time you want to be bored to death, ask again."

Her hair was pinned up on top of her head, but several curling tendrils had fallen down around her face. She looked, thankfully, more like a teenager than a bride, more like the irrepressible—irresponsible—girl that she was.

"Bye Abby," she called, then regarded him thoughtfully. "Mitch Hamilton in blue jeans and a T-shirt. I'm surprised!"

Not nearly as surprised as I was to see you in a wedding dress. "Are you?" he said dryly.

"I would have guessed pleated casuals—Dockers, and a sports shirt. You know, the golf and country club uniform."

"I don't golf." He was watching her closely. Despite the playful banter, he detected a faint nervousness that he was almost positive could not be totally attributed to ripped pants.

"You don't? I thought golfing was mandatory for doctors, lawyers and accountants."

Somehow the picture she was giving was of people who were *boring*. Why did he feel so insulted that he'd convinced her with such ease that he belonged in that category? His rebel wanted to convince her otherwise, grab her and kiss her until she was senseless, but his rational mind won out once more. Thank God.

"Did you have some business you wanted to discuss with me?" He recognized his stuffiest lawyer voice.

"Hmm. Do you think we could go grab a coffee somewhere?" she asked.

"Sure."

In the car, his rebel took over the wheel and drove like a complete idiot, just to show her well and for good, that he was not *boring.*

She apparently was used to wild rides. After an intensive study of her fingernails, she made a few bright comments on the weather and the houses they were going by. He couldn't very well carry on a conversation and drive like a maniac, and soon, when she discovered the conversation was going to be largely one-sided, she retreated into blessed silence.

Blessed because he liked the sound of her voice. The sunshine in it made his life seem country club dull, as if he lived under a gray cloud.

He picked up the speed a bit and cast her a look. Not the least bit nervous at taking the curves at this speed. No gasps, use of the imaginary braking system, or bracing. In fact, she looked pensive, turned inward. Why did he suspect she was rehearsing what she wanted to tell him?

He drove them down the coast a ways, to a little coffee shop that was built right on some rocks overlooking the pounding surf.

Not because it was *romantic,* he told himself, though he admitted now that they were there, that it was.

He told himself he had only chosen it because he suspected at this hour on a Sunday, it would be nearly empty, affording them the privacy necessary for a counselor-client appointment. Not that she was his client.

He realized he hoped she never would be.

The waiter made eyes at Brit, which she didn't seem to notice, and gave them a private table at the window overlooking the wind-tossed waves.

Brit took her seat, again looking everywhere but at Mitch. She gave the waiter a smile of such brilliance that the poor man would have married her on the spot if she asked him.

Thankfully, she didn't.

Instead, she spotted some seagulls dropping clams to break the shells on the rocks, and chattered about that for a few minutes.

"You had some business you wanted to discuss with me?" he asked.

"I should have asked you what you charge, first," she said brightly, but he could tell she was coiled tighter than a spring.

"No charge."

"Oh. I don't expect that. At all. Mitch—"

"Look, if I end up doing some work for you, then we'll talk charges. Right now, I'm just going to listen to what you have to say."

She sighed, and looked like she was going to start talking about seagulls again. He gave her a warning look and she took a deep breath.

"I want out of the bakery. I want to know where I stand legally."

She said this with a certain breeziness, but when he looked closer he saw she was still having trouble meeting his eyes, he noticed a small tremble in her bottom lip. He knew, with something that resembled intuition, something he could have sworn five minutes ago he didn't have, it had cost her to come to him with this.

Cost her plenty in the pride department. It was only just over a week ago she had been proclaiming she was going to make that bakery into business-of-the-year.

"Why do you want out?" he asked, surprising himself again. The man he had been a week ago, the man who had told her not if she was the last woman on earth, might have reminded her of that business-of-the-year thing.

"Oh," she said waving a hand carelessly. "It's just not for me. Wouldn't you say I'm more a dress shop type?"

"But you weren't given a dress shop."

"Well, the gift is from a complete stranger. How could they know what type I was? It's so obvious a huge error in judgment was made. I was hoping I might be able to trade."

He had a vision of another Miracle Harbor business being dismantled and painted pink. "Tell me what's wrong with the bakery."

"I mean I don't have a doubt that I could make it a huge success, but I just thought a dress shop would suit me better. Or a jewelry shop."

He wondered if she had any idea what the inventory of a jewelry shop would be worth, or the kind of skills a good jeweler had.

"Do you think trading is a possibility?" she asked hopefully. "Even a remote one?"

"I'm not that familiar with the case, Brit, but I'll hazard a guess. No."

"Oh." She slid him a look. "Do you know who gave us the gift?"

"No. It's cloaked in secrecy. If I did know, I couldn't tell you."

"Wouldn't," she said.

"No," he repeated firmly. "Couldn't."

"Oh."

"I take it that things did not improve noticeably since I saw you Monday?" He hadn't been back, had been deliberately going into hiding at coffee time, so that his father couldn't drag him down there. It wasn't that he didn't want to get pressed into helping again. It wasn't that at all. The truth was he couldn't bear to see her bungling along.

The man he had been a week ago might have delighted in it.

"What's wrong, Brittany?" he asked. She looked away from him, and he reached across the table and took her hand, making her look at him.

"Oh," she said. "Nothing's wrong."

"My job is to ferret out truth," he said quietly, "and you, Brittany are not that good at lying."

A wink of something bright behind one of her eyes. She ducked her head, drew in a deep breath and then looked at him. "I don't know if I like it or hate it that you see what no one else sees," she whispered. "Everybody else has always believed me when I fibbed."

"Why are you fibbing?"

"Because I'm mortified."

He heard the truth and listened carefully.

"My feet hurt all the time, my nails are broken."

She held up a nail for him to look at, he suspected because she didn't want him looking in her eyes anymore.

"And?" he probed, not falling for it.

She gave him a disgruntled look, tucked the broken fingernail away, and said, "Could we talk about my dress shop? I thought a few designer clothes, a funky atmosphere. This town *needs* something like that."

"I want to know what's going on at the bakery that has made you want to throw in the towel."

"It's not how I thought it was going to be," she said, her voice losing the breeziness, sounding small and broken.

"In what way?" he asked, knowing he was finally at the heart of the matter.

"I thought it was going to be fun. Instead, I can't stand the sound of the door opening. It means more people and more dishes and I usually haven't even got the tables cleared from the last bunch and nobody buys torte. Last week I put some tables outside and a man came and told me I have to have a special license for that, and then all my tablecloths blew away.''

He watched her closely as the floodgates opened further.

''Luigi is mad at me about some wretched pipe, a lady screamed at me because her stupid birthday cake had the wrong color of icing on it, people walk out when I can't get to them fast enough, if I make the wrong change they act like I did it on purpose, and I wash dishes for two hours after I've closed...and I can't stand it!''

Why, when he had known this was where her business was going, did he feel so appalled to see her looking so...defeated?

''So,'' she said, failing entirely to look blasé, and looking embarrassed and scared instead, ''can you find me a loophole? Okay, maybe not a trade, but something to get me out of there and into a little dress shop?''

''I think this is kind of my dad's department.''

''I don't want to talk to him.''

''Why not?'' He really couldn't imagine anyone not wanting to talk to Jordan, *choosing* him over Jordan to talk to. Jordan was so sympathetic, and so diplomatic. Half the old biddies in Miracle Harbor dabbled in real estate just so they could go sit in his office and chat with him over the paperwork.

''Oh, Mitch, he's so distinguished and kind, and I just can't bear for him to know I've failed. Not,'' she said quickly, ''that it has to be a total failure. I've given it some thought. If I can't trade, what if I leased the bakery to someone else, like Luigi? I'm sure he'd be thrilled to get me out of there.''

Mitch registered that she thought she had failed. Mitch did not know what it meant that she had trusted him with this information, when she felt ashamed to even discuss it with his father.

But he did know that something in him rebelled against the idea of this woman, who was so full of fire and light, feeling like a failure at anything.

"Can you help me?" she asked.

"I think so," he said slowly, and quashed the look of relief that chased across her face by adding, "but not in the way you want."

"What do you mean?"

"I don't think you've given it a fair chance," he said quietly. What he didn't say was that if she walked away from that bakery she would carry that failure inside of her, surrender some of her beautiful fire to it, let it bow her shoulders just a bit, touch the proud angle of her chin.

It would change her in some fundamental way. From a girl who believed she could make anything happen to someone more realistic, more pragmatic.

Just like him.

God knew, the world had enough hims.

"But I have tried," she said, leaning forward earnestly, her eyes so wide he had to brace himself not to be drawn into her spell. Like everyone else in her whole life had been. "Mitch, I've tried."

"For a whole week?" he chided her.

She glared at him, which he found a distinct improvement over wide-eyed pleading.

"You don't know how tired I am! I wake up in the morning, and the first thing I smell is bread baking, and I hate that smell now because it means Luigi's been at work since four and he's already got two sinks full of dishes, and it's not his job to do his own dishes. So I go in an hour before the bakery opens, which is at seven, and put on coffee, and try to do dishes, and the phone starts ringing and then customers start coming in, and they leave messes on the tables. I have tried. *I can't do it. I can't.*"

"I think I might be able to help you out."

"I hope I heard emphasis on the *out,*" she said sulkily.

"I'm involved in an organization that helps teenagers who have had some scrapes with the law. Sometimes the hardest thing for these kids is to find somebody who will give them a chance, give them some work skills so they can start fitting into the mainstream, earning their own way."

"*You* work with troubled kids?"

He was not sure whether he should be insulted by the incredulous note in her voice.

"Yeah, I do."

"Why?" she asked.

He shrugged. "I was one of them once. And somebody helped me."

"Jordan," she guessed.

"That's right."

"What kind of trouble did you get in?" she asked eagerly.

"About every kind a kid can. What brought me to Jordan's attention was a stolen motorcycle."

"I knew it," she breathed. "You and motorcycles. I just knew it."

He wondered how. No one else in his world would have ever guessed. Certainly not Monica. Thankfully not any of his clients. "Could we get back to your situation?"

"Mitch, I think it's wonderful that you work with these kids, but I'm terrible with stuff like that. Kids don't like me. Not even my niece, Belle. Ask her."

His annoyance must have showed in his face, because she rushed on. "And I'm terrible at service work. Let's see. I've tried the candy striper thing, Christmas dinner for the homeless, and Toys for Tots. I always dress wrong, and say exactly the wrong thing, and people who have suffered misfortune like me even less than children. I feel so awkward around them, and then they know it—''

Her voice died away. He knew he looked disapproving and he didn't give a rat's whiskers.

"Okay," she said. "Here is the embarrassing truth. I don't think I can afford to hire anyone. I mean, I don't really understand the books that well, but my first week is looking like a financial disaster.''

"I can help you apply for a grant that would pay up to half of their salaries.''

"Really?'' She didn't look all that thrilled.

"Really. So you could hire a busgirl or boy to look after the dishes and clear the tables during your busy time.''

She looked slightly more thrilled at that. She was looking into his eyes for the first time since they had sat down. Her shoulders were coming back up, not carrying the weight of the world on them. She was beginning to smile.

And then the smile faltered. "Are these kids like, um, juvenile delinquents?''

He nodded, watching her closely.

"They've committed crimes?''

He nodded.

"Like what?''

"They're juveniles. Their records are sealed.''

"Could you give me a hint? Like are we talking murderers?''

"No. But just about anything else you can think of, from assault to theft.''

"How do I know they won't steal from me?''

"Do you trust me or not?'' he asked quietly, and was rewarded by a light that came on in her eyes that he was not sure he had done anything to deserve.

"Okay,'' she said, firmly, as if she were trying to convince herself. "I trust you.''

And the words felt like a gift sitting on the table between them.

The Monday morning coffee rush was over. Brittany felt a little resentful that she had survived another one. She had hoped by today, Monday morning coffee rush would be somebody else's problem. Luigi's. How had she let Mitch, that silver-tongued devil, talk her into giving it another shot? Hiring criminals?

What she'd really had her heart set on was taking the money from Luigi leasing her business from her, and opening the dress shop. There was a business right down the street for sale. No wonder. The frumpy clothes in the window said it all. But with a dash of paint, and an imaginative window display—

"Hi."

Brit looked up from rearranging the now seriously depleted doughnut supply. No chocolate mocha torte today. And no more until the water pipe got fixed, according to Luigi. Not that they needed more. Her freezer was full of tortes that had gone too stale to sell but that she couldn't bear to throw away.

A girl stood on the other side of the counter, shifting her weight from foot to foot. She had hair that had been bleached—badly—and her makeup was terrible, the heavy black liner under her bottom lid making her look shopworn despite the fact she could only be sixteen or seventeen. She was chewing gum, and wearing clothes that were faded, two or three years out of style.

"I'm Laurie Rose. Mr. Hamilton said I should come talk to you."

Her first criminal, Brit thought, eyeing the girl warily. Laurie Rose looked just plain tough, something hard in her face as her eyes wandered around the bakery.

Looking for things to steal? Brit wondered uneasily. Was

she allowed to ask the girl why she had been in trouble with the law?

But then the girl's eyes met hers before they skittered away, and Brit saw terror in them. Suddenly Brit knew Laurie Rose was terrified of being here, of being rejected, of being judged, and she knew she wasn't going to ask her anything about her problems with the law.

Do you trust me? she heard Mitch say.

"Hi, Laurie Rose," she said, and the gentleness in her own voice took her by surprise, as if she was handling one of her father's young horses, nervous and high-strung, so scared all they could think about was running. "Did Mr. Hamilton tell you I'm in a bit of a mess here?"

Laurie Rose shook her head, no.

Somehow Brit knew the key to this girl would be to show her that everybody had vulnerabilities. She took a deep breath and plunged in. "I'm brand new to the bakery business," she said. "And I'm terrible at it."

Laurie Rose blew a surprised bubble, then cast a little furtive look at the cluttered tables behind her.

"I get behind and I need somebody who can help me keep up—especially with the dishes and the tables." She gestured at the litter of coffee cups and crumb-filled plates on the tables.

"I could do that," Laurie Rose stammered, and suddenly she didn't seem so tough at all.

"But it's only for a few hours a day," Brittany warned her. "And it doesn't pay very much."

"That's okay."

"How come you aren't in school?"

"I'm dumb." The hardness was back.

"Oh," Brit said weakly.

"But I can do dishes. Geez. As if I ain't been doing that all my life."

"Oh."

"But if you're looking for a genius, I'll just shove off. It doesn't matter to me."

But somehow Brit could tell it did. A great deal. "When could you start?"

The girl looked astonished. "You're going to hire *me?*"

"Why not?"

"Mr. Hamilton said you'd ask me all kinds of questions, like where I worked before and what my grades were like at school and stuff. He made me practice answering. I didn't think I'd ever get a job."

The thought of Mitch caring about this girl, coaching her, filled Brit with a strange sensation of warmth. Under that cold exterior of Mitch's was a heart. A good heart.

And somehow she had known that even before Laurie Rose had told her.

"Well," she admitted, "Laurie Rose, I don't know any more about hiring people than I do about running a bakery, but I'm in a pinch and if you can wash dishes, and clear and wipe tables, you could help me out."

"I've been arrested," Laurie Rose said, watching her closely, moving her gum from one side of her mouth to the other.

"Uh, well—"

"Lots."

"Oh."

"You can ask for what if you want."

"You know, Laurie Rose, I think I'd rather not know. If you want to tell me someday, that's fine, but for now my chief concern is getting the mess under control. How about if we try it for a week, and if we're happy with each other, you have a job?"

"Okay," Laurie Rose agreed, and then she smiled, and when she smiled it erased every bit of hardness from her face, and made her look young and hopeful and very beautiful.

"Good," Brit said firmly, "if you could start as soon as possible."

"Right now?" Laurie Rose said hopefully.

Brit smiled, too. "Somehow I was hoping you'd say that."

And suddenly Brit was so happy that she had decided to trust Mitch. Because money could not buy the look on that girl's face.

"Thank you, ma'am."

"If you ever call me ma'am again, you'll be fired," Brit told her. "It's Brittany, or Brit."

"But Mr. Hamilton said—"

"Just between you and me, Mr. Hamilton doesn't know everything."

"Well, just about," Laurie Rose defended him. And then they both giggled.

By Friday, Heavenly Treats was a different place. Laurie Rose attacked her duties with silent fervor. When she was finished doing dishes and clearing tables, she sought out surfaces to polish. The floors and table legs and display cases and windows gleamed. She was always early for work, and left late. When Brittany told her she couldn't pay her for her extra time, to please go home, Laurie Rose wrinkled her nose and said she liked it here better.

Brit's feet still hurt, but when she saw Laurie Rose taking on her humble duties with such enthusiasm, being so grateful to have something to do, she decided she could not complain. In fact, she was entertaining Business-of-the-Year notions all over again. The customers were happy and even Luigi didn't seem quite as grouchy as usual. He was very pleased about the condition of his bread pans now that Laurie Rose had taken over the task of cleaning them.

Brit was only sorry that Mitch had not dropped in to see how things were going, though he had called once to let her know her application for a grant had been approved, and that Laurie Rose's on-the-job training would be half paid for.

His voice had been deep and businesslike.

She had found herself hoping he would say something personal, keep the conversation going, but he hadn't. Who could blame him? So far she had failed to impress him. A lawyer would not be looking for a wife who sported strands of pink in her hair, and blew the seat out of her pants! If she just had one more chance, she could show him what she really was. She was certain of it.

But there was no sign Mitch planned to give her one more chance, which meant she was going to have to put that ad in the paper again, but she didn't want to.

Lawyers from his office dropped by the bakery all the time. But Mitch did not. Farley Houser came in one day, and asked her, almost shyly if she would like to go out for dinner one night.

Why did she turn him down? When he would obviously be so accepting of her foibles?

"Brit, you aren't going to throw out that food are you?" Laurie Rose asked in horror as they put things away Friday night.

"Well, it won't be any good by Monday."

"Could I have it?"

"Of course," Brit said.

"For the teen center," Laurie mumbled, and Brit knew it was the first time the girl had lied to her. She suspected, suddenly, achingly, there was no food in Laurie's house.

She wanted suddenly to take those thin shoulders and hug that poor scared girl who jumped every time there was a loud noise behind her.

But she didn't know how to do that, so she said instead, "Laurie Rose, could I show you something about makeup?"

And so behind the locked doors of the bakery, she sat Laurie Rose down in a chair, and they stripped her makeup off her face and started brand new.

"My own sisters won't let me at them," Brit said regarding Laurie's face with satisfaction once she was done. "Are your ready?" She handed her a mirror.

Laurie stared into it. And then she whispered, "But I'm beautiful."

"Didn't you know?" Brit asked her gently. "We could do something with your hair, too."

"Could we?" Laurie breathed. "Please? There's a dance at the teen center tomorrow night."

Giggling like two teenagers instead of one, they tried several hairstyles, until they both agreed on a casual clip-up, and Laurie Rose reluctantly went home.

That night Brit went home and didn't feel as exhausted as she had felt. She felt warm and wonderful.

And her sense of wonder increased when she came home to a blinking light on her answering machine and a message from Mitch Hamilton wanting to know if she'd like to join him in chaperoning the teen center dance the following night.

It was her one more chance, and Brit planned to make the most of it.

Chapter Five

Mitch hung up the phone and then sat for a moment, staring at it as if it was a strange monster that he had never noticed before, that had appeared out of nowhere to squat menacingly on his desk, sending him commands.

Call her. Call her. Call her.

Call her and what, he'd asked it back. Talk? About?

Of course, he could ask her about the bakery and Laurie Rose.

It was embarrassing. He was a thirty-year-old man, who had earned his various badges of honor, both on the streets and in the courtrooms, and he didn't know the first thing about talking to a woman.

Except that wasn't true. He had absolutely no problem talking to 99.9 percent of the women he had to talk to.

It was *her.*

He analyzed it, comfortable analyzing, and came up with a satisfactory answer. He was uncomfortable contacting her because Brittany Patterson was a woman as intent on getting married as he was intent on staying single.

That was why it was so scary, he realized with a sensation of relief. Because even *talking* to her was dangerous.

She was a woman looking for a husband.

And he was a man looking for—

Well, the sad truth was he had no idea what he was looking for. He didn't feel like he'd been looking for anything, until she'd arrived in his life like fireworks going off at exactly the wrong time.

Until that moment he had considered himself a man completely content. He liked his job, he liked the town, he liked his glass-and-cedar house that overlooked the ocean. And he liked working with the kids at the Miracle Harbor Teen Center.

A common thread running throughout his life might be the control factor, but he wasn't prepared to say that was a *bad* thing.

But he had not felt much contentment or control since her lips had branded his at that wedding, two weeks ago this Saturday. He suddenly found his controlled mind drifting to the most adolescent of thoughts. The color of her eyes, the softness of her lips, the swell of her breast, the curve of her hips. Even the thought of the pink paint in her hair could make him smile, usually at a moment when smiling was absolutely the wrong thing to do.

"Smiling Your Honor? *Me?*"

Okay. So he'd given in. Called her. It had been a relief to get her answering machine, even though a glance at his clock told him she should be home from work, and made him wonder which husband candidate she might be off interviewing.

That thought crossed his mind often, too. Was she actually meeting some of those jerks, and did she have enough discernment to know they were really only interested in the bubble bath part, no matter what they said? And how about old Farley, walking around the office whistling, even after he'd lost the baby pool? Thoughts like those, crowding his mind, making him frown, even after they had announced dear old Millie won it.

"Scowling, Dad, *me?*"

It must have been that momentary flash of insanity, when her phone was ringing and Mitch was wondering if she was with Farley Houser, that had chased the bakery and Laurie Rose from his mind, because when he got her answering machine, he hadn't mentioned either of them.

No sir. He'd mentioned the dance he was chaperoning tomorrow night.

As if a repeat of dancing with her was going to help him keep any small measure of his sanity.

Not to worry. She wouldn't go. Who was he kidding? Brittany Patterson at a teen center dance as a chaperone? She was probably more accustomed to dances where swimming pools were filled with champagne—or food color— where live bands played, and Barbra Streisand put in an appearance and made-to-order confetti was blown around the room all evening.

Besides, she'd said her feet hurt the last time he saw her. Women with sore feet and an ounce of sense did not go dancing. He had nothing to worry about. Unless he *analyzed* the ounce of sense part.

His phone rang, and he felt his nerve ends leaping. He leaned forward and studied the call display, a machine he considered the best invention of the millennium, and felt everything within him tighten up.

B. Patterson, his caller I.D. read.

That would be her.

If he didn't answer it, he could distance himself from her rejection, not have to think of something to say to make it seem like he didn't care.

Which of course made him face the fact that he cared. He picked up the phone. "Yeah?"

"Hi, Mitch."

Pretend you don't know who it is. He couldn't. He was incapable of playing those kinds of games. "Hello, Brit."

"Are you still at work?"

"Just about wrapping up."

"Don't you have a life?" Her voice full of playfulness and sunshine, as if she had not been standing behind a counter serving people doughnuts all day instead of playing tennis or surfing or whatever rich girls from California did with their days.

Funny. I was just asking myself that very thing. "Yes, I have a life."

"There's no need to sound so grim about it."

"How would you know?"

"Mitch, have you had a bad day?"

He fought the sudden aching in him to tell someone at the end of the day all the little things that had happened. The funny things and the sad things and the in-between things. To share the little pang of fear he had felt when his father forgot what he was saying midsentence, to laugh with someone that his secretary had won the baby pool instead of Farley who had the majority of the squares.

"No," he said sharply. "I've had a great day."

"Me, too. A great day, a great week, thanks to you sending me Laurie Rose. She's terrific."

"I'm glad you like her." *Where were you after work?*

"I'd love to come to the dance with you tomorrow night. Will you pick me up? What should I wear? Do they have a theme?"

"A theme?" he said weakly.

"You know. Like Sadie Hawkins or something."

"Don't you wish," he said sourly.

Her laughter pealed across the telephone line. "Actually I'm taking a break from looking for a husband at the present moment, though I want to forewarn you, you are going to see me at my very best tomorrow night. Not a trace of pink paint. No man's shirt hiding a rip in my pants.''

He was thrilled about her news that she was taking a break from her husband-hunting, but he decided it might not be wise to let her know. He had a feeling his approval might bring on a new hunt, and a new intensity. Not a single bachelor in Miracle Harbor would be safe.

Except maybe him. The one who had told her not if she was the last woman on earth.

''As far as I know, no theme. A few kids and a CD player.''

''Laurie Rose grabbed some doughnuts that we were going to throw out, but I had the awful feeling they weren't really for the dance.''

He pondered the sadness in her voice, the fact that she had the sensitivity to pick up on that.

''She's from a big family,'' he said. ''There's not much money.'' And just like that, the funny little ache inside him seemed to ease.

It hit him like a bolt of lightning. *He was lonely.*

And he didn't want her to know.

''Actually, you might not like the dance. It's not exactly the kind of outing you're accustomed to,'' he said, and held his breath. Waiting for her to back out. Hoping she would and hoping she wouldn't at the very same time, which his lawyer's mind told him was impossible.

His rebel snickered.

''I can't imagine how boring life would be if we just did things we were accustomed to. I certainly wouldn't be running a bakery today!''

He smiled, reluctantly. God, that girl could pry a smile out of him. ''You actually sound happy to be running your bakery this week.''

''Well, if not happy, at least not looking for an exposed pipe to throw my rope and hangman's noose over.''

He laughed. "I'll pick you up. Tomorrow around eight."

"Do you want to dress up?" she asked. "You could be a riverboat gambler, and I could be a can-can girl. That would probably liven everything up, give the kids a laugh."

"No, I don't." Firmly.

"Mitch, has anyone told you, you are just a bit of a stick in the mud?"

"No."

"It's about time they did."

Don't ask her. But he did. "You don't know how to do the can-can, do you?"

"Oh, sure. I was a can-can girl on the gold fields in my senior year play. That's why I have the dress. Somewhere."

Somehow he couldn't even think of her in a can-can dress, all frilly petticoats and long legs, without feeling a storm of desire.

As if she knew exactly the effect she'd had on him, she set down the phone with a laugh, and without waiting for him to say goodbye.

He looked at the receiver. A riverboat gambler and a can-can girl? A stick in the mud? The thing about her was there was never going to be a dull moment. And he *liked* dull moments. The thing about her was that he was never going to be completely in control.

Not when just thinking about her in that outfit made him feel like this.

If he had no intention of marrying her, and he certainly didn't, why was he pursuing this relationship? Was taking a girl to a dance pursuing a relationship, exactly?

The truth? He found her irresistible. Something about her beckoned to him, as surely as the flame beckoned the moth.

And just as surely, he was dancing with fire, flirting with it, and even enjoying his duel with the flame.

But on Sunday, he would take a firm grip on himself,

take his life back. No more wayward thoughts about her lips, no more listening to a phone telling him what to do.

He'd take her to the dance tomorrow night, and that would be that. And he meant it.

I wonder, his rebel mused, ignoring him, *if she'll wear a red dress. I love red dresses.*

"Abby, do you think I could borrow your red dress?" Brit had asked her sister when she'd called her later that night. "You know that little number with the spaghetti straps that you were wearing the night I arrived in town? The one that had Shane eating out of the palm of your hand? Or I should I say panting helplessly at your hem?"

"Brit," her sister sounded horrified, "I never wore the dress to make Shane pant. What a terrible thing to say."

"Of course you wore it to make him pant," Brittany said. "You're just too much of an innocent to recognize your own motives. Whereas me—I recognize my own motives all the time. And I want that man panting, completely in my power."

"What man?" Abby asked. She sounded like she pitied him.

Brit was surprised she found herself reluctant to name Mitch. She realized, with a shiver of shock, that somehow she didn't want what was developing between them to be a big game of catch-the-man. Which surprised her. She had never had such scruples before.

On the other hand, if a woman honestly thought a guy was great looking, and she did, there was nothing improper about wanting him to reciprocate the feeling. He just had to sit up and take notice. Too bad he'd nixed the can-can girl outfit. It was guaranteed to make every man within a million miles sit up and take notice—and that was before she kicked her heels up over her head.

Still, her mission was to erase those damaging first impressions. First the pink paint, and then Scarecrow-of-the-Year in Shane's shirt and her ripped pants.

And what exactly did she think was developing between them?

To be truthful, she wasn't sure. She only knew when she thought of him her heart did this strange excited two-step within her chest. She longed, a dozen times a week, to pick up the phone and talk to him.

"Mitch, guess what just happened? A lady special ordered a chocolate mocha torte for her husband's sixtieth birthday."

"Mitch, Luigi smiled at me today. He's got a gold tooth."

Silly to think he would care about such mundane little details.

She realized, startled, that she was lonely. And then, with even deeper surprise, that she had always been lonely.

Of course, having sisters helped, but even so—

"Stop," she ordered herself. "I hate those worry furrows. Yuck."

She completed her preparations and she looked at herself in the mirror with satisfaction. She looked ravishing. The pink gone from her hair, the speckles from her arms, the red dress perfectly fitting, passionate, nearly as good as the can-can dress. She twirled, and liked how the dress flared around her slender legs. She'd have to do lots of twirling when she danced tonight.

She tried to picture Mitch's face when he saw her, his blue eyes getting that darker, smoky look to them that made her heart beat double-time in her chest.

He was going to see the real her, this time. Flawless. Sophisticated. Fiery.

She stopped, midtwirl and listened. Was there a sound coming from the bakery, below her?

She listened harder, then bolted for her door not even

bothering with her shoes. Key in hand she flew down the back steps, then let herself in the back door of the bakery.

She had hoped she was hearing wrong, but there was no mistaking the sound of running water.

She reached for the light switch but nothing happened. Cautiously she stepped inside. Water swirled around her feet up to her ankles. Ice-cold water.

"No," she wailed, and waded in, squinting in the darkness. She slogged her way to the sink, but both taps were turned off. As her eyes adjusted to the darkness, she became aware of a stream of water pouring down beside her, coming from the roof. She moved toward it, looked up.

In the inky darkness she could see the pipe above her, spurting water, and then without warning the pipe burst and poured over her, a torrent that nearly knocked her off her feet. She shrieked, surprised, indignant, and just a touch hysterical.

Oh, God. What now? This was one of those moments when a woman really needed a husband. When she was paralyzed and didn't have a clue what to do—

"Brit?"

Her first thought, completely irrational, was how could this be happening to her? From sophisticated and utterly gorgeous to a drowned rat in the blink of an eye.

The dress felt like soggy paper clinging to her, and her hair was plastered to her face and dripping in her eyes.

Her second thought, even less rational than the first, was that it was her own fault. She knew he appeared as soon as she even thought of husbands.

And her third thought was how glad she was that Mitch was here. How could she be upset he was here and glad he was here at the very same time? It seemed impossible.

"Back here," she called, her teeth already clacking together. She could see his dark silhouette, outlined by light from the open door, as he moved into the kitchen. Strong, calm. A man who knew what to do.

"Don't move."

But did he always have to be giving people orders? Don't move when a ton of water was falling on her head, ruining her hair and her sister's dress? She slogged toward him.

"Stand still, Brit, I mean it."

Something in his voice made her listen. The faintest note of fear? She skidded to a halt. "Why?" she asked.

Silence. He moved off into the darkness, and then to her relief he was coming through the murkiness toward her and he scooped her up and pressed her soggy body against him.

"The breaker blew, thank God," he said, and held her as if he would never let her go. The wet dress provided no barrier at all. She could feel the hardness of his chest against her cold nipples, his body felt so warm against her that she thought she might ignite.

He was holding her as if he was helpless to do anything else, looking at her in exactly the way she had hoped the red dress might make him look. But it couldn't be the red dress, which was a complete soggy mess. A match for her hair, which hung dankly around her ears, and trickled water down her neck.

Why were men always such a big, bloody mystery? It would be so nice if they could just be uncomplicated, like women.

"The breaker?" she asked, into his neck. Her panic subsided completely. The curve of his neck was so strong, sensual somehow, the texture of his skin beneath her cheek like steel wrapped in silk.

And he smelled good. Clean and tangy, like soap and pine forests. And something else. The scent—indefinable, mysterious, wonderful—of a man. His arms around her were powerful, as if he had the strength to protect her from anything, and his breath in her ear was calm and steady.

"If the water had gotten into any of the outlets—"

She felt him shudder against her. "Are you telling me I could have been electrocuted?"

"I'm telling you next time you see a building flooding call a plumber. Or the fire department or 911."

All sensible suggestions that made far more sense than wishing for a husband.

"Or me." His voice was an intimate growl in her ear.

"You're always telling me what to do," she whispered against his neck.

"Somebody has to do it," he said mildly.

"I seem to have survived this far without it."

"A miracle."

"And here I am in Miracle Harbor." And it did feel like a miracle. To be in his arms. To feel his protection of her. Never mind the water pouring out her roof and climbing steadily up the walls.

He put her down near the door. "I'd better find the water shutoff or we'll be treading in this stuff soon."

She wanted to tell him to never mind the damned water shutoff. Did he know there were times and places when he really didn't have to be so practical?

He turned from her, and then slowly turned back. His eyes narrowed in the darkness. "Is that a red dress?"

"It was," she said mournfully.

"Go get changed," he said.

More orders.

He took a slip of paper out of his pocket and wrote a number on it. "This is Laurie Rose's home number. Can you call her? Tell her what happened. I think they'll have to cancel the dance. I have the key, and you and I were the chaperones."

"The dance! We can't make the kids miss their dance because of this."

"If anybody knows life doesn't always go according to

plan, it's these kids. They'll be okay with it. We'll do it a different night.''

He was canceling over a little bit of water, when she had been dying to dance with him again.

"Look, I can just change, and we'll run over there—"

"If we can get some of the water out now, we might be able to save your business."

"Save my business?"

"Can you imagine what will happen if this water starts to seep under the floors, gets in the electrical outlets, between the walls?"

"Oh, God."

"Spoken like someone who loves her bakery. I'll see if I can find us a pump. Go call Laurie Rose. I don't mind canceling the dance, but I don't want those kids standing outside thinking yet another adult has let them down."

Brittany raced up the stairs, called Laurie Rose, who sounded stricken. Not that the dance was canceled, bless her heart, but that the bakery had been damaged.

Then she took off the red dress, which looked disgustingly like red crepe paper that had gotten wet, and flung it in her bathtub.

Anything she put on was going to get wet and possibly ruined, so with a sigh she pulled on her paint clothes, unflattering as they were, rolled up the jeans to the knee, and headed back down the stairs to her disaster.

"I think my Dad has a sump pump," Mitch said. "You want to come with me? We'll run over to his place?"

Of course, she wanted to go with him.

But she was not the carefree girl she had been two weeks ago. She knew now she didn't always get to do what she wanted.

"No, I'll stay and start bailing water."

Stunned by how acutely she felt his going, felt it the second his calm presence left the room, she slogged through the bakery and found some of the empty plastic pails that the baking ingredients came in. She began the hard and tedious job of scooping up water, slogging over to the sink and dumping it.

Mitch was back in minutes, with a pump and a lantern, and soon an eerie light was washing over the room. It looked awful, like a ship getting ready to sink, the water swirling, papers and pails and other odd items floating by in mysterious currents. He waded in without hesitating.

"Your clothes are going to be ruined," she told him. "Golf and country club acceptable, too."

He gave her *the* look, rolled up his sleeves and went to work. He took charge with complete ease, and within moments had an extension cord hooked up to her upstairs outlet, and had the long hose for the pump going out the front door and into the sewer.

Scooping up a basket that floated by her, she was watching it with satisfaction as the water level began to lower.

Then an enormous old black car careened around the corner and screeched to a halt in front of the building. It had no fenders, and only one working headlight. It was crammed to the roof with tough-looking boys.

Looters, she thought, as they began to tumble from the car.

She felt Mitch arrive at her shoulder, and the fear left her somewhat. And then she glanced at his face and saw he was smiling, his arms folded over the broad swell of his chest.

"Hiya, boss."

He greeted each of the boys by name.

She tried not to stare too long at the tattoos and chains and pierced body parts.

"This is my friend, Ms. Patterson," Mitch introduced her.

"Brittany," she corrected him.

They eyed her with wary shyness that lasted about three seconds, before the biggest one proclaimed her *hot* and gave Mitch a sly look and a thump on the arm.

Hot, she thought, as they pushed by her, following Mitch into the shop. She touched her bedraggled hair, looking down at her paint clothes. She wondered, with sudden horror, if her makeup was running.

"Pete, do you have a license?" Mitch sternly asked the one who had been driving.

Pete ducked his head. "Laurie Rose told us what happened. It's an emergency."

She could see Mitch was trying hard not to smile.

"I'll drive you home after," he said. "You ready to go to work?"

"That's why we came."

She trailed in after them, and watched with growing awe the respect Mitch commanded from these boys.

They had come to help her, a complete stranger, and somehow that belied their tough looks, as did the way they looked at Mitch.

A few moments later, an old Volkswagen van pulled up, and at least twenty more kids piled out of it, laughing and shoving, armed with buckets and mops.

"We've come to help," they called as they waded through her front door.

"Thanks," Mitch said. "If we can save introductions for later, I'll give you each a job. Daisy if you could make sure everyone has a bucket. And Ralph, if you could start picking up the stuff floating around and see what can be saved, and what can't. Cameron, get the chairs up on the tables. There she is. Laurie Rose, are you an angel?"

She blushed softly.

"What have you done to your hair?" he asked, and Brittany felt a lump in her throat, that in the middle of all this, he found the time to notice, and knew it would matter. "It looks great. Okay, battle stations."

It was then that Brit noticed, that like she had been, moments ago, they were all in their best clothes. And yet they waded unhesitatingly into her mess. She could not miss the looks they shot at Mitch. Respect. Admiration. No, more. Love.

These kids loved this man who was so good at appearing hard and distant and cool. They saw right through him.

And when she saw him leaning toward a boy with purple hair cut in a Mohawk, listening intently, then throwing back his head and laughing, she saw right through him, too.

Soon her bakery was ringing with laughter and kids chasing each other through the water, and throwing buckets at each other, and somehow the work was getting done, too, the water disappearing off her floor and down the drains and out the door.

A wall of water hit her, as if she wasn't wet enough. And when she turned on her attacker, it was Mitch, his eyes alight with laughter, his shoulders shaking, his clothes absolutely plastered to him.

With a cry she chased after him with her own half-filled bucket, the kids shouting, "Come on, Miss Brit. Get him."

He dodged over that still soaked floor like a quarterback, using bursts of speed, managing dazzling changes of direction. Finally he slipped, and hit the floor, and she threw the contents of her bucket over his head, and saw the white of his teeth as he laughed up at her.

He reached out and caught her ankle and pulled her down on top of him, and for a moment she thought he was going to kiss her.

And so did the kids, because they were hooting and calling encouragement.

And then silence.

One of the kids swore. "As if that's a sound I don't recognize."

They all froze as the wail of sirens drew closer, and then a huge spotlight was on the window.

And a tinny voice ordered them out, with their hands up.

Brittany stared out the window in shock. Even though she was nearly blinded by the light, she could see the policemen behind their police car doors with guns leveled at her picture window.

Mitch was off the floor, fully serious. "Stay here," he ordered her and the kids, "and don't any of you move a muscle."

His hands folded calmly on top of his head, he went out the door and stood in the blazing light. Afraid of nothing. His great pride and self-composure in the set of his shoulders, the stance of his long powerful legs.

Brit started breathing again when she saw the police lower their weapons, and come forward smiling, but she could see some of the kids looked uncomfortable, others defiant. She was thankful when the police just put their heads in the door, shone their lights on the floor and then left again.

Within minutes the Miracle Harbor Fire Department showed up to check for electrical fire hazards.

"Are they always so helpful?" Brit asked.

"They're all single," Mitch teased. "Probably read your ad and couldn't wait to get over here to check you out."

"They wouldn't have known it was me that placed that ad!"

"Ha. There's no such thing as anonymity in a small town."

It was after midnight when to great cheering, the last of the mopping was done. The damage, at least in the flickering light, looked minimal. The fire department had advised her not to turn the power to the bakery back on until an electrician had checked the wiring.

"All right," Brittany called. "Everybody grab a drink from the cooler, and upstairs to my apartment. I'm making popcorn for the crew, which is a chintzy way to pay such a hardworking group—"

But they didn't seem to think it was chintzy. The kids were piling up her stairs, thrilled to be invited into her apartment.

"They're soaked," Mitch said to her in an undertone. "Do you know what you're doing? They might ruin your furniture."

"I guess you've never seen my furniture," she said. "Besides, they've probably wrecked the best clothes they own. For me, a complete stranger. Do I know what I'm doing? You bet I do."

She counted them. Twenty kids, laughing and talking, sprawled on her furniture, looking through her CD collection and making faces at each other.

"Pete, you ever heard of a band called Mozart?"

"Nah. How about The Rankin Family? You ever heard of them?"

"I think they guest-starred on *Sesame Street* the other morning."

She went into the kitchen. Mitch followed her. "You're soaked," he said. "Why don't you go and get changed, and I'll make the popcorn?"

"Can anybody else get changed?" she said to him. "I will not accept preferential treatment. The pots are under there."

And soon every burner of her stove was red-hot and Mitch and her were trying to shake four different pots of popcorn and smiling at each other as they overheard the comments the kids were making about her music in the next room. The CDs they had sampled so far had lasted an average of thirty seconds.

"Hey, I like that one," Mitch called. "Peter, Paul and Mary. It's classic."

Silence from the living room, and then howls of laughter as Peter, Paul and Mary hit the discard pile.

Mitch eyed her. "You don't seem like a Peter, Paul and Mary kind of gal."

"Shows what you know. Remember, you thought I wasn't the handy kind either."

"I've got to stand by that. You can't even make popcorn."

"I can—" She pulled a smoking pot off the stove.

"Hey, guys, give that one a chance. It's Bette Midler," he called. "Hey!"

Bette Midler discarded.

They delivered the heaping bowls of popcorn, and the girls put on Celine Dion singing the theme song from *Titanic* while the boys groaned and made faces.

After they had listened to the Celine Dion CD all the way through once, and the kids had cleaned up the popcorn dishes without being asked, Mitch told them it was time to go.

"Pete, I'll drive you home. And I don't want you going out in that car again without your license."

Pete mirthfully produced the license, obviously thrilled that he'd fooled Mitch into thinking he didn't have one.

"Got it yesterday, boss. You didn't think I'd do nothing illegal did ya?" He turned to her. "Miss Brit, we'll have the dance next week instead. You come, okay?"

"Um, I will if I'm invited."

"Didn't I just invite you?" Pete said, confused.

"She means by Mr. H.," Laurie Rose said in an undertone, and elbowed him in the ribs.

"Oh." Silence, and then the girl named Daisy began to

clap, and they all joined in. And they began to chant. "Ask her. Ask her. Ask her."

"Okay already," Mitch said, holding up his hand. "Miss Brit, would you do me the honor of accompanying me to the Teen Center next Saturday night? Barring tornadoes, floods, blizzards and other natural disasters?"

"I certainly will," she said.

Then giggling and hooting, and the kids went out the door, and the room was suddenly empty save for Mitch and Brittany, and Celine Dion.

"Do you think they left because of the music?" she asked, gazing at him. He looked wild and reckless in his wet clothes, his hair falling down over his forehead. She remembered a kiss interrupted.

"Nah. They left because you ran out of popcorn."

She laughed, aching suddenly with weariness.

"Does anything with you ever turn out the way a person plans it?" he asked.

"I hope so," she murmured.

He cocked an eyebrow at her.

"Because I planned to dance with you tonight, Mitch Hamilton, and I'm not letting you go until we do."

They both knew he was closer to that wide open door to her apartment than she, and that he could leave if he wanted to.

But his eyes darkened and he moved toward her.

"The kids like you," he said. "They don't like everybody."

"That's good," she said huskily.

"Go to bed," he told her, lifting a strand of her wet hair away from her face. "You're shaking, you're so cold and tired."

"Aye-aye, boss. As soon as I've had my dance."

"Do you know what you're doing?" he said as he gathered her close to him.

"Um-hmm," she said, "Exactly."

"You're freezing."

"I'll warm up in a minute."

She sagged against him, felt him gather her close, felt suddenly exhausted and safe and content in the circle of his arms, as he swayed gently to the music.

"You were right," he said softly, and she felt his lips touch her forehead. "You promised I would see you at your very best tonight, and I did."

She was not sure anyone had ever said anything so wonderful to her. "Mitch," she murmured thickly, "are you sure you won't marry me?"

And she smiled when he said nothing at all.

Chapter Six

"Thanks for the warn—er, for calling, Laurie Rose. Oh, sure. I can't wait." This was a lie, but Mitch had a sudden dignity-saving brainstorm that might give him the upper hand for once. He shared it with Laurie Rose. "You like it? You want to run it by Brittany? Tell you what. I'll do that myself."

Whistling, he hung up the phone, put on his jacket and headed down the hall.

"Dad, are you coming for coffee?"

"Not this morning, son. I'm—" Was his dad blushing? "—meeting Angela this morning."

Mitch bit back his normal comment about her being meddlesome and looked at Jordan. He'd been widowed just after Mitch graduated from law school, Helen succumbing to a long battle with breast cancer.

Even today, when Mitch thought of his adoptive mother he felt the same lump of emotion in his throat. Helen had been a class act. Childless, she had welcomed Mitch and his siblings into her life as if the four young ruffians and a baby were just what she had waited for all her life. Her china broke and her priceless rugs got mud on them, and she never stopped acting like having a ready-made family dumped on her in her later years was a miracle beyond measure.

Sometimes, she'd almost succeeded in making him believe it. Almost.

Now, looking at Jordan, Mitch realized his intense loyalty to Helen made him feel prickly about Jordan's new relationship. And he realized that would be the last thing Helen would have wanted.

Jordan looked happy. Wasn't that what mattered when you loved someone? Not controlling their lives for them, making their choices for them, but wishing them every happiness.

He sighed. "Have fun, Dad. Give Angela my best."

Jordan looked up at him with surprise, and then looked deeper at Mitch. He smiled. "Where are you going for coffee?"

"Where we always go," Mitch said, daring Jordan with his eyes to make that a big deal, but Jordan didn't. His secretive little smile was even worse.

The day was warm and sunny, a perfect day in early May, the air sea-scented, the flowers beginning to bloom in breathtaking abundance.

Mitch realized he had never been good at stopping to smell the roses, and he wondered at himself that he seemed to be seeing the world with brand-new eyes today. With freshness and eagerness and hope. He didn't even find it necessary to analyze what he hoped for.

He slipped into the bakery, only letting the door open halfway so that the bell above it would not jangle. A table or two had not been cleared, but other than that it looked like a place of relative calm this morning—if one could ever feel calm in the midst of so much nerve-jangling pink.

Brit's back was to him, and he considered his deep appreciation of her from this particular angle. He decided, self-protectively, his appreciation of her was part of his fledgling stop-and-smell-the-roses personality. He went up to the counter, and he noticed she was wrestling with a filter on a coffee machine. It gave way suddenly, and he saw her staring down at the front of her apron with dismay.

"Lady, I want three dozen jelly doughnuts, and I want them now. And the jelly better be grape."

She whirled, ready to hiss and scratch like an angry kitten, and then her face broke out in a reluctant smile. She tried, with absolutely no success, to flick away some of the wet grounds smearing her front. The view of which was better than the back, despite the apron.

"I was beginning to think you were boycotting me. Is it because you've been put to work every time you come through that door?"

"No, it's because of the paint. It hurts my eyes."

"Get sunglasses," she suggested unsympathetically.

"What are you behind on today?"

"Can you knead bread?"

"No."

"I guess you're allowed to just be a customer, then. But don't let it become a habit."

"So, as a paying customer, what are my options?"

She wrinkled her nose. "Honey-glazed or chocolate doughnuts and plain old American coffee. Miracle Harbor wasn't quite ready for me."

"I think maybe you have that effect wherever you go."

She stuck out her tongue. It was delicate and a shade of pink he actually liked. It made him think naughty thoughts about leaping the counter.

"Actually, I dropped in because Laurie Rose just called me," Mitch said, with the cool control of a man who had never once in his entire life entertained the thought of leaping a counter to steal a kiss.

"Oh?" Eyes widened innocently.

"To tell me there was a *theme* for next Saturday's dance."

"Really?" Pure astonishment in that voice.

"Don't try and sound the innocent with me," he said dryly. "I know exactly where she got that idea."

"She isn't even here today! It's her day off. You of all people should know it's *innocent until proven guilty.*"

"Hollywood Comes To Miracle Harbor," he said grimly. "Everyone required to dress as their favorite movie character."

"Oh," she breathed, as if this was the first she'd heard of it. "The possibilities. Marilyn Monroe, Bette Davis, Elizabeth Taylor. I don't know how I'll ever choose."

"You won't have to. A twist has been added to the original plan. If it's a couple going, the man gets to choose the characters."

"No! I never told Laurie Rose—"

"Ah-ha!"

She gave up trying to wipe off the coffee grounds, folded her arms over the offending area, and frowned at him. "So, I suppose you get to pick."

"That's correct."

"Have you given it any thought yet?"

"Of course."

"I would make an absolutely stunning *Runaway Bride.*"

Didn't she ever think of anything else? "You and I are going as Mickey and Minnie Mouse."

"Mitch! Come on. Don't do this to me. I beg you. How about *Beauty and the Beast?* I'd make a magnificent Belle. I could have my mother FedEx my prom dress."

He made himself look unimpressed, but he liked the way

she screwed up her features when she was thinking hard and fast.

"Or, if you must do cartoons, how about *Lady and the Tramp?*"

"That would only be fun if *you* got to be the tramp," he said.

She was beginning to look stubborn and sulky. Then she brightened. "I've got it, Mitch. I've got it. You won't be able to refuse this. *Gone with the Wind!* Me Scarlett, you Rhett. Abby could do a few renovations to the prom gown and—"

"Nope."

"You have a nasty streak."

"Not at all. I'm just making a statement about being a stick in the mud."

"*Grease,*" she breathed. "I could be Olivia in the final scene. I seem to recall black leather. Tight."

"Tempting, but no."

"All right, in desperation I will offer you a bribe. A year's supply of jelly doughnuts *with* grape filling. In exchange, I will be Stands-with-a-Fist, to your Dances-with-Wolves."

"I don't really see myself as the Kevin Costner type."

"Oh." Her eyes got very wide. "Of course not. Why didn't I see it sooner. *Braveheart.*"

"You've been thinking of nothing else ever since you planted this idea in that poor impressionable girl's young mind."

"I have not."

"You'll make a great Minnie."

"The insurance adjuster was here this morning," she said sweetly.

"And?" He knew this change of subject would have a point.

"Not too much damage, though the walls are badly

stained around the bases. They're going to pay for me to have them repainted."

"That's great."

"Not that you are suggesting there was anything wrong with the old paint, of course?"

"I've always wondered what was under that Humphrey Bogart poster."

"Don't look! Mitch, I was thinking painting would be a great work project for your kids."

He was actually taken aback it was such a good idea. He could handle her when she was just plain gorgeous. When she was bright and bubbly as a glass of champagne. But sometimes he caught glimpses of something else, and he knew if he explored that he would be in over his head before he knew what had happened to him.

"That's brilliant," he congratulated her.

"I know. And you know what's even more brilliant? I'm not awarding you the contract unless you choose different movie characters. Anything else will do. But not Mickey and Minnie Mouse. I will not be seen with mouse ears."

"No problem." Thank God. There was something in it for her, after all.

"I knew you would see it my way."

"You bet. See you Saturday night, Madame Mim."

"Madame Mim? Does that sound as delicious as I think?"

"Have you seen *The Sword in the Stone?*"

"The Sword in the Stone?"

"A Disney animated about King Arthur as a young boy."

"King Arthur," she breathed, approvingly. "But I don't remember his woman being named Madam Mim. Oh, no! You can't mean the fat little witch who duels with Merlin."

"Oh, yes."

Understanding dawned on her face. "That's not what I meant. You have to choose new characters that *I* like."

"You said, and I quote, *anything else will do.*"

"But that's not what I meant!"

"It's still legally binding, a verbal contract, even if you didn't say exactly what you meant."

"I meant for you to chose Scarlett and Rhett."

"But then," he said smoothly, "It really wouldn't have been my choice at all."

"You can't be serious. Madam Mim, a chunky little witch with a bad temper."

"Always wanted her own way, that woman."

"I see you have backed me into a nice little corner. If I say one more word, it will only make me seem ideally suited for the role. Are you this sneaky in court? Do you back people into tight little corners that they can't get out of?"

"I don't like to think of it as sneaky. Clever. Canny. Perhaps with a little cunning thrown in."

"Madam Mim," she said, with a shake of her head.

"That's correct. You get to be Madam Mim to my Merlin. It would be lovely if you would be gracious about it." A date, he thought. He had avoided wording it so formally.

"Gracious," she muttered. "It seems to me she turned old Merlin into a toad or something worse."

"No problem. I'll bring two costumes. At toad-time just give me the word. The kids will adore that."

"Don't you understand?" she howled. "I want to be sexy and gorgeous!"

"Don't you understand?" he said softly. "You can't stop being that, no matter what you are wearing, or pretending to be." And he meant it.

Her mouth fell open, and while she was speechless, he said, "I'll have two sugar doughnuts and a good old American-style coffee. By the way, I think I can talk Hamilton,

Sweet and Hamilton into donating the paint, but only if it's a nice shade of pale blue. Restful. Relaxing. Conducive to digestion.''

"I'll think about it. Farley would have let me be Scarlett.''

"How do you know?" He felt his eyebrows pulling down, and he deliberately straightened them.

"Oh, he calls from time to time.''

"If Farley had picked a movie, he would have picked *Seven Brides for Seven Brothers,* only Farley would have played all seven brothers.''

"The poor man has terrible taste in women,'' she said sympathetically.

He stared at her, and felt that familiar desire to strangle her. It was obvious to him the opposite was true. Any woman who chose a man with Farley's kind of track record had terrible taste in men.

But he narrowed his eyes and saw Brit was trying to make him jealous. Or trying to get her own way. Or more probably, a little of both.

He had to stay one step ahead of this girl.

And he knew, sipping his coffee, that could be a full-time job.

"Abby, I hate this costume," Brit said glumly. "Hate it. Would you please quit putting so much effort into it?"

"Me like," Belle said firmly.

"Traitor," Brit said and stuck her tongue at her niece, who rewarded her by laughing robustly.

Abby was sewing mop strands into a huge black, pointed hat. Patched. "It's a wonderful costume. I wish Shane could see it. He'll be back in a minute. Hilarious. How much time do I have?"

Brit didn't want her handsome brother-in-law seeing her in this getup. She rearranged the enormous water balloons that were fastened to the inside of the voluminous dress Abby had found at a secondhand store. She gazed down at her brand-new figure with mournful dislike.

"I always thought I wanted to be voluptuous. Be careful what you wish for, my mother always said. Do I have to wear this pillow in the behind? Are you and Mitch conspiring to make me the ugliest old sow in all of Miracle Harbor?"

"Brit! Lighten up!"

"Light up," Belle agreed happily.

"Oh. Easy for you to say. You come to Miracle Harbor, and get to play Cinderella, transformed for the ball complete with Prince Charming. You get the happily-ever-after part. I come to Miracle Harbor, and get Cinderella in reverse. From princess to pauper. Calluses on my feet and hands. Pink paint in my hair. Nearly drowned in my own shop. Asked to go to the ball as Madam Mim. No glass slipper for me."

"When did you become such a stick-in-the-mud?"

"It's rubbing off on me. It probably has something to do with the company I've been keeping."

"Have you been seeing lots of him, then?"

"Oh, don't get your hopes up. I'm as far away from getting married as I was three weeks ago. He came in for coffee and doughnuts every morning this week, but he's just trying to discourage my other suitor."

"What other suitor? For a girl who's as far away from getting married as you were three weeks ago, you don't seem to be lacking in company."

"My admirer is Farley Houser, a distinguished lawyer also with Hamilton, Sweet and Hamilton, who would have let me go to the dance as Julia Roberts in the *Runaway Bride*."

"Anyone can see you are not the Julia Roberts type."

A door slammed and Shane came in, sweating from running. Looking gorgeous. Belle screamed, "Daddy!" and he picked her up and tossed her in the air with easy strength.

"And I am the Madam Mim type?" Brit demanded of him.

"I don't think you are supposed to go to a costume party as yourself," her brother-in-law told her mildly. It occurred to Brit that he was so enamored with her sister he probably wouldn't notice if she were sporting a second head! Shane announced he and Belle were off to make mudpies and they left.

"Well," Brit said, miffed, "I might as well have gone as Julia! I could have borrowed your wedding dress. It would have been sumptuous."

"Brit, you've always seemed to have such a wonderful sense of humor. Look in the mirror. It's the most delightful costume!"

"Don't you get it?" She looked in the mirror and scowled. She looked short, fat and funny, not exactly the impression she wanted to make. "My point is my dreams are not coming true! And maybe they never will."

"Oh, darling, don't say that. If ever a girl could make the whole world fall in love with her, it would be you. And that's even dressed as Madam Mim."

"Me? Make the whole world fall in love with me?" She almost strangled on the lump that rose in her throat. She forced herself to respond breezily. "Oh sure, though come to think of it Mitch said something similar. Not that he used the L word, of course."

"He said something similar?"

"And don't read anything into it. I may marry Farley— next week—just to spite him. Mitch, not Farley."

Abby ducked her head suddenly.

"Are you laughing at me?"

A knock at the door.

Brit sighed with great suffering. "Give me the damned hat."

Abby went and opened the door.

Mitch looked resplendent in floor-length, flowing black robes with silver stars sewn on them. Somehow his dignity was completely intact. In fact, he looked powerful and mysterious.

Brittany glared at him, and put on the hat. It fell over her eyes, and she shot him a black look from underneath it.

He looked at her and chuckled, and then laughed and then howled, especially when Brit moved toward him and Abby's cleverly placed balloons and pillows all bounced and swayed.

"That is the greatest costume I have ever seen," he finally gasped.

"Humph. You won't be so sure when the boobs break on you."

"I've been all wet around you before."

"'Bye Abby. I won't say goodbye to Belle. I don't want her to have nightmares."

"I see you have the character down to perfection," he said. "Fierce. Cranky. Maybe even dangerous."

"Be quiet, or I'll turn you into—"

"I'm shaking. You'll turn me into what?"

"Farley Houser."

And that wiped the grin off his impossibly handsome face. Fast.

She had decided to let her extreme annoyance about being forced to make a public appearance as Madam Mim show in bristling silence as they got in his Mercedes.

The car smelled exquisite. Of leather, but *his* scent, clean and masculine and heady, had found its way into every nook and cranny of the confined space.

They were soon leaving the quaint and beautiful Miracle

Harbor that was all she had ever seen. Gone were the rambling shingle-sided houses, the manicured yards and painted picket fences and climbing rosebushes. The streets they drove down now were lined with boxy, wartime houses with few trees and flowers, and then even that deteriorated.

Mitch drove them across an invisible line into a different world. The houses became small and shabby, crying for paint, patches of lawn gone to weed. Windows were boarded up or broken, fences had fallen down, rusting metal cars served as yard ornaments.

She forgot she was Madam Mim, looked bleakly out the window. Which of those houses did Laurie Rose live in? Pete? Daisy? She could feel Mitch gauging her reaction, even though he said nothing, didn't even appear to be looking at her.

"Is this where it is?" she asked when he pulled the car over.

He nodded. "The part of Miracle Harbor most in need of the miracle. The part the Chamber of Commerce doesn't want anyone to see."

He came around to her door, and opened it.

The street seemed dark and abandoned and *mean.* In a movie, spooky music would be playing and danger would be lurking down that shadowed alleyway.

"It can't be safe to leave your car here."

"My car is safe here. And so are you."

She took comfort in that, looked in his face and sensed a truth. He might wear fine clothes, at least when he was not dressed as a wizard, and he might drive the best of cars, but right underneath the surface was the cool command of a man people did not mess with. She felt suddenly safer, more protected, than she had felt since her parents had broken it to her that she was on her own.

Ridiculous to feel that way. The man had forced her to wear a costume that allowed her no dignity at all.

"What's that?" she asked of the hulking, rotting building that squatted on the end of an equally rotting wharf. Rows of windows, high up, were all broken.

"It's the Jones Brothers' cannery. This used to be a fishing town, many years ago."

"It's so ugly."

His mouth was a grim line. "It was even uglier when it closed."

She glanced at him. "Why?"

"People worked there. A terrible job. Bad hours, the stink of fish, hard physical labor. But a terrible job is better than no job. My mother worked there, until it shut down. We lived right over there."

She looked at where he was pointing.

"You lived there?" she whispered.

"Until I was thirteen."

There was no way to align the shack he was pointing at to the man who stood beside her, so confident, so at ease, so sure in the world. The house was tiny, she suspected just one room, and everything about it seemed to sag—the porch, the roof, the windows. The shingles had blown off part of the wall, and tarpaper flapped in the wind.

She glanced at him. He was watching her, his eyes half-closed in assessment, his face remote. She guessed him to be thirty, but couldn't imagine this house looking much better even seventeen years ago.

She knew instinctively he would not want her pity, and so she was silent, some part of her telling her to wait.

Suddenly, she was even glad of the costume.

To show up in this neighborhood in a Southern Belle hoop dress, or a wedding gown worth thousands of dollars would have been slapping these kids in the face.

He had known that.

In fact, when she looked at his eyes on her they seemed to be asking her if she was ready to be more than she had ever been before.

Of course she knew the answer was no.

He glanced at her, a trace of a smile pulled his lips upward, and turned on a light in his eyes that she would have just as soon not seen. When that light winked on in his eyes it made her want to believe in all kinds of things she had long since outgrown—fairy tales and forever after.

"Just so that you know," he said softly, "that you're being accompanied by a man from the wrong side of the tracks."

She registered that he had just told her something about himself. Something intensely personal for all that he had said it casually. She didn't know what to say that wouldn't chase the moment away. And then she did.

"Just so that you know," she said, just as softly, "where you came from doesn't interest me nearly as much as what you've made of it. Sometimes very good things come from bad."

"I guess that's true. Knowing a few street fighting tactics hasn't always been a bad thing."

She felt both oddly moved by his confiding in her, almost ready to forgive him for making her into Madam Mim instead of Marilyn Monroe.

A man in an undershirt came out of a house across the street, scratched himself, watched them with a cold curiosity that made her shiver.

Mitch saw the man, and raised his hand in casual greeting. She looked back in time to see the man wave back, grinning toothlessly. Harmless.

"Where's the teen center?"

"Just up the block. It would have been hard to park any closer to it."

It was just another old house in a row of old houses,

only it was a bright place amongst this squalor. A cheerful mural with butterflies and sunshine decorated one gray-shingled wall, a few meager flowers tried desperately to grow in the flower bed, the thin grass was mowed, the porch swept and inviting, curtains hanging in the windows.

A hand-painted sign hung at the gate.

It said Hope.

"The kids did it themselves," he said, holding open the gate for her.

He took the stairs two at a time, and fitted a key into the locked door. The door swung open and he went in.

She hesitated on that threshold, feeling like if she crossed it with him, her life would change forever.

Then she plunged forward.

The inside was as cheery as the exterior. A large room held a pool table and a few sofas. The walls were painted sunshine-yellow, and white drapes hung crisply at the windows. A big window with no glass in it looked through to a neat kitchen.

She felt something in this room that nearly took her breath away. A spirit. A feeling. Of energy. Of—

Hope. "This neighborhood is teeming with kids," he said quietly. "Poor kids. No designer clothes, no Corvettes, not much of anything. The kind of kids that you read about in the paper, because they end up on the wrong side of the law with depressing regularity. Drugs, theft, petty crime. Graduating all the time to bigger and better things."

He was changed, somehow, standing in this room. Not so hard and cold. A passion in him that touched some part of herself that had always been cool and untouched.

No, not always.

That had whispered to life when his lips touched hers, when he held her.

"These kids," he continued, "need one thing more than anything else. Something to hope for."

She looked at this fresh-scrubbed space, and could feel the pride they took in it, could feel their hopes and their dreams clamoring around her, and felt afraid of being given something so sacred and fragile.

And she realized that was what made her the very same as those kids.

She longed for something to hope for, too.

Then the kids began to arrive, and furniture was being shoved back against the walls.

She was grateful all over again that Mitch had nixed her grandiose ideas for a fancy costume before they had even had a chance to fully hatch. She would have been as out of place as an angelfish in a tank full of guppies.

The kids' costumes were so simple it was nearly heart wrenching. A cheap bandana, obviously new, transformed one into Maverick.

Blue jeans and T-shirts on lots of the boys, claiming to be Bruce Willis in various venues. The girls, in miniskirts, were almost unanimously *Pretty Woman.*

The girls swarmed around her *loving* her costume. Her hat began to make the rounds. Many pleaded to try on her "implants," which Abby had thankfully sewn into the dress.

"Have you guys ever heard of The Chicken Dance?" she asked, suddenly feeling a surge of happiness, of belonging. It was a feeling her apple-red Corvette had not succeeded in giving her, or her Chloe pantsuit, or her Vivienne Westwood dress. "Believe me, you're going to love this."

And then she saw Mitch looking at her, a tiny smile playing around his lips.

And she knew why he had chosen Merlin.

Because he was a wizard.

A great one.

Because without half trying, he seemed to have cast a spell on her heart.

Chapter Seven

"No, no, Weldon. Hop forward once, then, *ouch.*"

Weldon, a hulking boy with extreme acne and a criminal record checkered with all sorts of interesting incidents, was looking down at Brit worshipfully. His normally hard expression had been completely chased away by laughter.

Mitch had actually been doing quite a bit of laughing himself. Brit, the belle of the ball, even in pillows and rags, knew how to have a party. Her giant Madam Mim hat had come completely loaded with obsolete CDs.

In three hours she had taught the kids to Chicken Dance. And him, too.

She taught them The Butterfly, and the Polka. Right now, she was working on the Bunny Hop. The kids usually put up their toughest front to strangers, but she had melted their resistance to her ideas about having fun in about two seconds.

And his, too.

There was just no combating her infectious laughter, her enthusiasm, her energy—her bossiness!

"Forward *hop*, back *hop*, right leg, *kick*, left leg, *kick*. I think we have it!" The line collapsed behind her in a hopeless tangle.

"Mitch, was that you?"

And she didn't tolerate any lollygaggers either.

"I tried to tell you, two left feet."

Mitch managed to untangle himself, and went to her, and looked down at her shining face, and felt something move within him.

Something gigantic. The first brick had just fallen out of the wall around his heart.

"I think," he decided abruptly, "we need to judge the costumes, and have the last dance. Some of these kids have a curfew." He didn't add court-ordered.

"Oh, goody," she said. "I can be the judge, can't I?"

"Why not?" he said. He didn't add it would be a scary thought being in court presided over by her. Judge Judy, only with a little less edge and a lot more looks.

"You're just saying that so I don't turn you into a toad."

"Absolutely."

She turned from him, looked around, and called the room to order. "We're going to judge the best costumes now."

And somehow she knew to pick Bobby McGiven, with his downcast eyes and his slumped shoulders as the best Bruce Willis there, and Amanda Potter as the best *Pretty Woman*, when it was so painfully evident she was anything but.

It was a measure of how far these kids had come that they cheered heartily for Amanda and Bobby. The prizes? Brit handed over her Chicken Dance and Polka CDs. Amanda and Bobby gazed at them as though they had received treasure from the queen. Not, he suspected, because they were going to listen to the music ever again, but because they probably had not been on the receiving end of very many unconditional gifts in their lives.

That was what she did—she turned the ordinary into the extraordinary.

"Last dance," he called.

The boys were around her thick as thieves, pleading with her to pick one of them for the last dance.

Considering his crumbling defenses, it would be absolute insanity to push those boys aside, and take her hand, and look deep into her eyes, but that's exactly what he did.

"She saved the last dance for me, guys."

She really was Madam Mim, but she hadn't used her charms to turn him into a toad after all. Being a toad would have been easy in comparison to this.

Wanting to look into her eyes forever. Actually wanting to feel this strange and delicious warmth she made him feel.

A delighted awareness of being alive, of vibrating with life.

He pulled her close, and every feeling he was having intensified. He smiled when the girls put on the theme song from *Titanic*. A song about love overcoming every obstacle, finding its way, not being thwarted, crossing time and space to find the enchantment of one special person on all the earth.

A song of great and soaring passion and tenderness that made him yearn for…something.

That yearning fulfilled by her body pressed into his. Or somewhere in there was her body. He pulled her a little tighter, wanting to feel her against him, feel her energy—

The water-filled balloons popped with such force that dancers on either side of them were hit with water.

The kids howled with fiendish pleasure.

"Never mind," she said, and pulled him back into her. "What's a little water between you and I?"

Now, an hour later, the kids were gone, and he felt, as he locked the door to the clubhouse, as if he didn't want to let her go. Wasn't ready. Couldn't.

He rehearsed what to say all the way down the walk to his car, and even in it, after he'd pulled away from the curb.

"Ah," he felt like a shy boy with the prom queen, "do you want to go for a drink or something?"

"No."

"Okay." There, she'd rejected him. She just wanted to go home. That would teach him to ever take a chance with his heart. Put the bricks back up, man.

"Mitch!"

"What?"

"You could try offering me an alternative."

"Pardon?"

She sighed heavily, an obvious indication that he was hopeless in the romance department, which he already knew. "I'm not going to go out for a drink dressed as Madam Mim, with my implants dribbling down my chest."

He laughed, relieved, confused by his relief, thinking with all the brickwork he was doing tonight he might want to consider a career in masonry. "Where would you like to go, Madam Mim?"

He thought she might suggest going home and getting changed, and then hitting a nightspot—which would be awkward because he hadn't had a social life for so long he had no idea which clubs were good and which weren't.

But instead, she looked through the windshield, up at the stars, and hugged herself, and said, "Do you know a nice quiet beach somewhere? We could sit in the sand, and listen to the ocean, and look at the stars."

"It's cloudy." He could have kicked himself, caught there in that place where the bricks were half in and half out, and he wasn't at all sure where he wanted them or what he wanted to do.

She sighed again, which he took to mean he was hopeless, but before he managed to shove the brick all the way back in, she said, "It wasn't the stars, precisely. The ambience of the beach at night."

Ambience. A word that almost rhymed with romance.

But beaches, he knew. Especially the quiet one right beneath his house. He changed direction smoothly, tried to find safe ground, a subject that wouldn't require a whole lot of brick shuffling. Which meant her search for a husband was off-limits.

"The kids had fun tonight, Brit."

"I know. So did I. Did you?"

He wondered if he had ever had fun like that before. He tried to think of a time when he had laughed until his sides hurt, given himself over so thoroughly to silliness. He could not.

"It was okay," he said, deliberately understating it. "These dances usually aren't quite that successful."

"Really? Why not?"

"No theme. No chicken dance. No polka." *No you.*

"So what do they do at them?"

"Those who are unattached kind of look wistfully at each other, and those who are couples end up on the couches, making me a very cranky chaperone."

"You? Cranky?"

"Don't rub it in."

She smiled. "Well, the kids adore you, cranky or not."

"Adore may be wording it a little too strongly." He pulled onto the shoulder, and parked by the entrance to a little-known public beach. His house was the next one up the street, but he didn't tell her. He shut off the engine.

"Adore is not too strong. I was there. I know what I saw. My little Laurie Rose has a bad case of hero worship."

"*Your* little Laurie Rose." He was smiling again, this time at the unguarded tenderness in Brit's tone. "You're good for her. She's come an amazing distance in the two weeks she's worked for you. She even looks completely different. From poster girl for juvie hall to wholesome and fresh, eager.''

"Makeup," Brit said. "A girl has to know how to make the most of what she has."

He wondered, with surprise, if Brit had a wall up, too. Because he knew the progress Laurie Rose was making did not have a thing to do with makeup.

It had to do with being cared about.

He got out of the car and opened the door for her, a girl who knew how to make the most of what she had, even dressed as Madam Mim.

"Mitch? I really like your kids, but—"

"But?"

"I don't want to talk about them anymore."

"What do you want to talk about?"

"You."

"Me?" He felt her slip her arm through his, walk beside him on the shrub-lined path that would open up in a few yards to the beach. He contemplated how right that felt, her arm in his, her slight weight beside him.

"I want to hear all about that boy who stole the motor-cycle."

"Why?"

"Don't you know? Girls just adore bad boys."

"Well, they shouldn't," he said gruffly, but his rebel was repeating, *adore.* He told his rebel, firmly, that she obviously liked that word, she tossed it around so carelessly.

They went out onto the beach, and she paused on a rock and looked up at his house. He had left a few lights on, and she took in a breath.

"Mitch, isn't that the most beautiful house you've ever seen?"

In the daytime it was evident it needed a fresh coat of cedar oil, but at this time of night it looked beautiful, the huge A-shaped wall of windows splashing golden light over the rocks.

Without waiting for him to answer, she kicked off her shoes, and sank down in the sand. She patted the place beside her, and pulled the pillow out of the backside of her dress. "I'll share," she said.

He sank down. And when he felt her shiver, realized her dress was wet. He could invite her up to his place. The thought seared into his brain. His rebel started jumping up and down in gleeful anticipation.

But the decent guy, the guy who was trying to set such a good example for those kids, the guy who was trying to leave behind a past with lots of sordid moments in it provided by his mother and her latest boyfriend, could not invite her home. He knew bringing her home, in close proximity to his bedroom, would be a very bad idea.

Not to mention a way to blast that wall down, never mind the slower brick by brick method.

Instead, he stripped off the wizard's robe, and wrapped it around her.

He had jeans on underneath, anyway. His rebel thought she was admiring his pecs, and he flexed them just in case.

And then he found himself telling her about his early life, and his brothers and sister.

About his Mom, the town drunk.

He could not believe he was telling anyone this, or the way she listened, so solemn, her eyes on the ocean, but her hand in his making him feel like he would tell her anything.

"So," he said, "I guess that's why I seem so cranky to you. Maybe cranky is the wrong word. I like to be in control, because so much of my world growing up wasn't. But, I know I have this rebel inside of me that I'm scared to death to let out."

"Really? What do you think he'd do?"

Kiss you until neither of us could breathe, or think, or say no.

"Who knows?" he said blandly.

But she suddenly looked him full in the face, not willing to let it go. "Steal a car, rob a bank, mug an old lady?"

"No! But something wild and crazy and out-of-control, that I'd regret for the rest of my life." Or glory in. Something so strong it could disintegrate bricks as though they were made of dust.

"You see, Mitch, I don't see it that way at all."

He'd ask her what she knew about rebels but he had the unfortunate feeling she had written the book.

"How do you see it?"

"That rebel in you helped you survive. He knew exactly how to meet your needs, when no one else would. He knew how to try and fill all those holes within you."

He said nothing, staring out at the ocean, feeling the truth of those words, and not minding the truth as much as he had thought he might. With a kind of stunned shock, he realized that she saw such a deep truth about him, a truth others who had known him so much longer had missed.

"And I know," she continued softly, "because I have that same person inside of me. A wild girl, who drives too fast and wrecks cars, and can never seem to get enough excitement. The last few weeks have tamed her a bit, though."

He smiled. "I didn't really see that tonight."

"Maybe," she mused, as if he hadn't spoken, "it's from being adopted that I never quite felt satisfied. Or loved. Or accepted. I always felt this strange desire to prove things. Do you think wanting to be the center of attention all the time is about wanting to be good enough?"

"Is that how you felt? Like you weren't good enough?" An echo of the boy he used to be. Poor. Uneducated. Wondering why on earth Jordan and Helen loved him so, wondering when he would let the mask slip and let them down.

"Don't get me wrong," she said softly. "My mom and dad did their best. But they weren't really kid people. Sometimes growing up, I wondered if they adopted me because it was the fashionable thing to do. Have this cute little girl to haul out in her cute little designer dresses that matched Mommy's. You know Mitch, they wanted to love me. They longed to. But nothing in their world taught them how.

"I have to stop this," she said, suddenly. "What am I thinking? I'm spilling my guts. I'm telling you things I've never told anyone. It's the moonbeams. The magic. I'm stopping now."

"Don't stop," he whispered, and he meant it.

"Mitch, I never stopped longing…"

"I know."

"You do, don't you?"

"Yeah."

"The love of my own mother. It has haunted me, that longing. It sits inside me and weeps. Finding my sisters has filled part of that longing, for me."

He was seeing something deeper behind the vivacious front she showed the world. The fact that something sat inside her and made her want to weep filled him with a deep longing to hold her, to dry those tears, to fill the rest of that longing within her.

Instead, he just said, his voice soft, "I know exactly what you're saying."

She smiled shyly. "So, I need to listen to my responsible adult side a little more often, and Mitch, you need to listen to that rebel every now and then. He helped you survive before. He probably knows exactly what you need now."

"I doubt that." And yet even as he said it, he looked at

her and wondered if that rebel was not leading him unerr-
ingly to what he needed most in the whole world....

"Why? What does he want? Right now. Right this second."

"To swim naked with you in the ocean." He was not
even sure where the words came from, some place so deep
inside himself, a place he had not visited often, a place of
utter honesty and utter vulnerability.

Her eyes widened. "Ooh," she said. "Somehow I knew
I was going to *love* your rebel."

Put on the brakes, he ordered himself. Oh, sure, put that
rebel in the driving seat and look what happened, brakes
off, flying pell-mell, hair straight back toward—what?

Bliss.

Because she was shedding Madam Mim, piece by piece,
and running for the ocean, a spec of white disappearing
into the dark night.

Wasn't she self-conscious about anything? Didn't she
have any sense of what was right and what was wrong?
Didn't she have any sense of propriety?

As if he didn't have enough for both of them.

He heard her hit the water, saw her white face bobbing
above the dark sheen of the waves, gentle tonight.

"Mitch," her voice floated up to him, "It's great. Come
in. It's only a little skinny-dip. It's not like you're committing a felony or anything."

He didn't need any more encouragement than that.

It was wild and untamed, a spontaneous moment, and his
spirit rose to it. When had his control, his need to be perfect, and safe, robbed him of these spontaneous moments
of sheer exhilaration?

He shed the jeans, and ran across the sand, dived cleanly
into the water. He surfaced a foot away from her, and she
splashed him, right in the eyes. By the time he'd shaken
the water clear, she was off. The first thing he saw was that

she could really swim. The second thing he noticed was between the inky darkness of the night, and the oily darkness of the water, he really couldn't see a thing.

Her strong crawl carried her out toward a small island of rocks just a little off the beach. He cut into the water behind her, and she led him on a merry chase, around the rocks and back toward the beach.

As if he shouldn't have figured it out by now. Nothing with her was ever as he thought it was going to be.

Somehow, he'd thought swimming together, naked, might be erotic.

Instead, he was having trouble even catching a glimpse of her. Every time he came even close to her, she would dive under the water and come up laughing where he least expected her to come up, throwing water droplets off her soaked hair.

And then, suddenly, she gave up, panting with exhaustion, the air around them ringing with her laughter. She was treading water, and her shoulders were white as cream, smooth and naked, just above the water. Suddenly he was looking into her eyes, the rest of her beautiful body cloaked by sea as black as velvet.

His treaded the water, and he reached out and touched a strand of her wet hair that had fallen in her eyes.

"Is your rebel happy, Mitch?" she asked softly.

"Delirious. Ecstatic."

She laughed. "Your rebel wouldn't even know words like that. Maybe it's you."

Her lips caught a shard of moonlight that peeped from behind dense cloud, and shone wet and inviting. And he leaned close, and touched his lips to hers.

Her lips tasted of salt and promises.

He slipped his hands down her body to her waist. Her skin felt unbelievable beneath his fingertips. Wet and slippery, delicate, perfect. Soft. Softer than anything he had ever felt.

So soft, it made him painfully aware that he led a life devoid of this kind of softness.

Her eyes were wide on his face, and he realized that suddenly she didn't seem so worldly, so confident. She looked a little bit frightened, as if she had gone a little too far, even for her, and didn't know how to admit it.

She was trusting him to do the right thing.

With great effort he took his hands off her, splashed her with the heel of his hand.

And then, just as she splashed him back, her face once again dancing with mischief and laughter, out of the corner of his eye, he glimpsed a cone of light moving across the beach.

His rebel said a word his lawyer *never* said.

"What?" she asked.

"Shhh," he said, nodding toward the beach.

"Who is it?" she whispered.

"The cops."

"Oh, God," she said, and as the powerful beam of light caught her she ducked under the water.

"Sir," it blared out over the bullhorn, "this beach is closed to the public at ten p.m."

He heard her surface behind him, could feel her breath in his ear as she peeped over his shoulder. He tried not to think how close her naked breasts were to his back.

"I'm not using the public beach," he called back. "I'm swimming from my house."

The light trained on his face.

"Mr. Hamilton?"

"Yeah."

The light turned off abruptly.

"Sorry about that. We found this heap of clothes here. No one else out there, sir?"

"No one but us...chickens."

She giggled behind him, and he could hear the low voices of the police saying something to each other now that they knew he was not alone in the water.

"Weird clothes, here," their voices drifted out. "It would almost seem like somebody came down here to do a little black magic. We'll just take them and put them in the trash."

She was sputtering with laughter now.

He was shivering he was so bloody cold. As the police disappeared he swam for his wharf, with her following.

Her teeth were chattering, too. "Why didn't you tell me this was your house?"

Why? Somehow he didn't want her intensifying her husband campaign because she liked his house.

Did that mean he wanted her to intensify it because she liked him?

"Come on," he said, hearing an edge in his voice. "We'll make a run for my house. I've got a spare key hidden."

"I'm not running around naked in front of you. Are you crazy?"

"It's a little late for Miss Modesty isn't it?"

"Skinny-dipping is one thing. Running around with no clothes on is quite another." She said this very primly.

If he argued the case with her they could both come down with hypothermia.

"Our clothes have just been disposed of by the police, Madam Mim. You seemed to think that was quite funny a few moments ago."

"Nerves," she defended herself.

"Any suggestions?"

"Yes. You run up to your house and get a sheet or something for me to wrap in."

"You know, I just knew I'd regret letting my rebel out."

"Mitch, don't say that. This is the kind of story we'll be telling our grandchildren someday."

"That would be assuming you and I had children, together, wouldn't it?"

"I see the lawyer is back, full force. I liked the rebel better."

"You would," he said and with one last glare at her, hefted himself up on the dock and began running up the stairs toward his house. His rebel loved it.

His lawyer felt he had had more dignified moments.

It would serve her right if he left her there, she thought, waiting until the dark swallowed him, then hauling herself up onto the beach, and finding a little shrub to hide behind.

She should be thinking only of the cold. Instead she was thinking, disgracefully, that Mitch Hamilton looked mighty fine with no clothes on.

What got into her around that man? She couldn't even blame it on champagne tonight.

His laughter had proved even more potent, making her feel drunk with happiness. That, and the way his eyes had sought her out in that crowded room. Then when he'd pushed her circle of junior admirers aside, and claimed her for that last dance with a certain masculine possessiveness, she had lost her head completely. Even the ill-timed explosion of the watery bustline had not dampened the fever that was growing in her.

She had nearly died of helpless delight when he had asked, ever so casually, if she wanted to do something else.

There it was. She was helpless against him. Helpless. And at the very same time she had the most powerful feeling that the whole world belonged to her and him.

How was it possible to entertain two such contradictory thoughts and believe each to be true with equal conviction?

But the moonlight swim had not been such a good idea.

A little too erotic, a step too close to lines that could not be stepped back from once they had been crossed.

Besides, now Mitch was going to think she was a wild girl, who did this type of thing all the time. The truth was she wasn't as worldly as she led people to believe. Not nearly as sophisticated. She had never been anywhere near a naked man before.

She had actually felt a little relieved when the white light of the police light had glared off of him. Because she didn't feel prepared for what was going to happen next, and that letting his rebel loose was obviously only leading one place.

It occurred to her that she had not fully considered what it might mean to marry a stranger to keep her bakery.

Somehow in all her plotting and planning, she'd forgotten the intimacy part, or naively dismissed it as less important and less powerful than it was.

And now that she had felt the wet silk of Mitch's body so close to hers, she somehow knew he'd spoiled whatever she might have felt for someone else.

The exhilaration of the swim was over.

She suddenly felt exhausted, confused, even a little frightened.

He came back down the stairs with a blanket. He'd pulled on a pair of shorts, but his skin was still beaded with water, his hair slicked back and springy from being wet.

From behind the bush she watched him, felt her mouth go dry with wanting him. Mitch was, simply, magnificent. Every muscle exactly where it was meant to be, not an ounce of flab, his body hard and beautiful in the moonlight that peeked unexpectedly from behind a cloud.

"Where are you?" he hissed.

"Close your eyes."

"Don't be ridicul—"

"Close your eyes or I'm staying right here."

With a sigh of long suffering, he closed his eyes, and she darted out from behind the shrub and into the blanket.

He folded it around her, and hummed a few teasing notes from "It Was An Itsy Bitsy Teeny Weeny Yellow Polka Dot Bikini." She tilted her head up and loved the laughter that sparkled in his eyes.

"Come on," he said. "I'll make us some hot chocolate."

She loved the feel of his arms closing around her, holding that blanket tightly to her, holding her. She loved the sound of his voice, gentle in her ear.

And she wanted to see his house. Oh, so desperately wanted to see all the little secrets it would tell about him. It would be neat as a pin, she guessed. Leather furniture? Chrome-and-glass coffee tables? Framed photos? Of whom?

She hungered for these glimpses of him, of his life, felt like she could never get enough or know enough about him.

She hungered to sit across from him, her soul dancing to the low music of his laughter, her heart beating to the passion in her eyes. She dreamed of removing a little fleck of whipped cream from the sensuous curve of his lip with her tongue.

She realized with sudden and staggering certainty that she had gone and done the most stupid thing of all. More stupid than getting pink paint in her hair, more stupid than trying to squeeze into those yellow pants, more stupid than encouraging his rebel out to skinny-dip with her.

She had fallen in love with Mitch Hamilton.

She wrapped the blanket tightly around herself. She couldn't go into his house with him. Not now. Not now that she knew.

How could she stop herself from flinging herself at him? Begging him to love her back?

"I need you to take me home," she said with quiet resolve.

"At least let me lend you some clothes."

She steeled herself against the question in his voice, the disappointment. "I'll be fine in the blanket. Can we get back to your car this way?"

He looked at her closely. "Brittany, what have I done?"

What had he done? Laughed with her. Danced with her. Rescued her. Played dolphin with her in the deep night-dark sea.

"Nothing, Mitch," she said softly. And that was true. He hadn't done anything at all. Had not even had the decency to fall in love with her when she had been so busy falling for him.

They trudged across the sand, and he silently opened the door of his car for her.

Within minutes, he was walking her up the back steps to her apartment, and said, hesitantly, "I really had fun tonight, Brit."

"Good."

"Thanks for making it such a special night for the kids."

She shrugged. "It was a special night for me, too." But of course he would never know the most special part of all.

Tonight, shivering under a blanket, feeling his arms, strong as bands of steel, close around her, she acknowledged she had fallen in love.

For the very first time. Bittersweet.

"Do you want to do it again sometime?"

Which? Swim naked or teach thirty teens how to do the Chicken Dance? Fall in love? Did it matter?

"I don't know. I'll think about it." It was as close as she could come to the flat-out no she had ordered herself to say.

Going into her house, she tripped over the blanket.

She couldn't even say goodbye gracefully.

Chapter Eight

Mitch folded his hands behind his head and stared up at his bedroom ceiling. A vaulted ceiling, done in tongue-and-groove red cedar. When he stared at it long enough the knots in the cedar seemed to have faces, a fact that he had been pleasantly unaware of for the majority of the four years he had lived here.

Now, he knew each of the faces on his ceiling intimately.

Intimately. Bad choice of words, when sleeplessness held him in its grip, when his mind wanted to drift back into velvety black water with her and do it all differently. He wanted to taste the salt on her skin until the world of waves surrounding them gave way to the fire neither of them could quench. He wanted to carry her in his arms up the stone staircase from the beach, through his house to this room, set her, wet and trembling on this big brass bed...

He groaned and looked at his bedside alarm clock. Three in the morning.

Thank God it was Sunday, and he didn't have to work in a few hours. Though there was nothing to make him think he would sleep any better tonight.

Impatient with himself he got up, padded out to his living room and opened the French doors onto his deck.

The night air felt cool and crisp against his heated skin. Below him the sea was still. He knew he was never going to be able to look at it again without seeing her swimming, without feeling the ache of all the things he might have said and done to keep her from leaving.

Without wondering what the hell he had done wrong.

There had been times when he had behaved terribly toward her. Times when he had been rude, sanctimonious, disapproving. Those times hadn't chased her away, and tonight after the most pleasant evening they had ever spent in each other's company, she'd run like the devil was on her heels.

Who would have ever guessed she would be the sensible one?

He wished he had a dog.

For companionship. An excuse to be out walking at this time of morning.

Sighing, he went back to his bedroom, looked at the clock, glanced wistfully at his rumpled bed, and then gave up. He pulled on an old pair of jeans and a hooded sweatshirt. By habit, he tucked his cell phone into the kangaroo pouch. Maybe tomorrow he'd look for a dog.

That might fill all these holes in his life.

He went out the door and began to walk, knowing he had to walk until he was too tired to think anymore, and knowing darn well dawn would be touching him before he found the nerve to go back to his empty house and his empty bedroom and his empty life to try to sleep again.

He followed the ocean, walking the beaches, climbing over rocks until his muscles ached, and his mind swam with fatigue. The shoreline brought him right to main street Miracle Harbor. The town slept. He continued walking, until he ended up in downtown, the ocean lapping quietly on one side of him, the dark storefronts on the other.

Without knowing why, he crossed the street, glancing in storefront windows as he went by.

He jolted to a halt.

That ring had winked at him.

Some fragment of moonlight had slivered through the jewelry store window, caught on the ice of a diamond, and it winked blue fire at him.

Ice and fire. Him and her.

He stared at the ring, transfixed. He was not a jewelry lover. He wore none himself, beyond the watch Helen and Jordan had given him when he graduated from law school. He had purchased a ring only once before—a monstrous thing clustered with fat diamonds that Monica had picked herself. That ring had cost him about half a year's salary. He'd told Monica to keep it when the engagement ended, and she had.

This ring was not like that ring.

It was pure simplicity, but in that simplicity was a beauty that showcased the fire captured inside that ring.

It was delicate, a fine band of gold, one solitaire that winked and danced and was fired with blue flame that reminded him of Brit's eyes.

A sudden image crowded his mind of that ring on her finger and he felt a shiver lift the hair on the back of his neck, the desire to buy it and give it to her was so strong.

The rebel taking over again, as if he hadn't done enough damage for one twenty-four hour period.

He helped you survive before. He probably knows exactly what you need now.

Only *needing* was something Mitch associated with weakness. When you needed you gave other people power over you. When you needed you were always disappointed.

Or could it be, he wondered, his weariness opening avenues in his mind that were usually firmly shut, that was the part of his past that he was ready to leave behind?

Maybe part of his maturing process was realizing a man could choose not to be alone, that that choice did not make him weak or needy. Just normal.

As if the word normal could ever be used in association with anything having to do with Brit Patterson.

Annoyed by the jumble of feelings in a mind that was so accustomed to order and clarity, Mitch pulled himself away from the jewelry display and continued down the street. He stopped at the pet store window, too. There were puppies in the window, sleeping. They were black and tan, and had huge paws to grow into. It looked like they might have shepherd blood in them somewhere. A man's kind of dog.

He picked out one, sleeping near the top of the heap, nestled into the warmth of his brothers and sisters. He tapped on the window, and the puppy woke up and gazed at him sleepily, yawned, and wagged his tail. No doubt about it. That dog would make a wonderful lifetime companion.

That choice carried with it no jumble of feelings at all. On Monday, he'd come get the dog. Forget the ring, and forget swimming in the darkness, and forget blue eyes, and wet strands of blond hair falling around a pale face. Especially forget about buying her that ring.

He had just turned back toward his house, ready at last to sleep, when his cell phone rang. It was a sound that filled him with dread.

Because that particular phone number ringing meant only one thing. One of his kids was in trouble.

He answered, and felt his heart break in two, not that he could ever let that show in his voice. His voice had to be calm and solid, and he made it obey him.

"Laurie Rose? You've got to slow down. Sweetheart,

stop crying. Take a deep breath. Another one. Okay. Tell me.''

He listened, and the weariness seemed to grow inside him, an enormous burden that he felt he could not carry alone. Did not want to, anymore. But by long habit, he let none of that show in his voice. When he spoke to her, he gave her what she needed. Calm. Composure.

She at least, would take comfort in the illusion he was in control.

''I'll be there right away. You're worried you woke me up?'' He marveled at her capacity to think of anyone else at the moment, then reassured her. ''I wasn't sleeping and I'm closer than you think.''

He disconnected the phone, took a deep breath, looked heavenward and asked for a miracle, and then headed back downtown to the Main Street Police Station.

Brit smacked the pillow furiously. Why didn't they let you take home pillows on trial before you committed to them? Damn lumpy thing. It was keeping her awake it was so lumpy. On Monday, she'd buy a new pillow and voilà no more sleepless nights for her.

It was, she told herself stubbornly, only the pillow that was keeping her awake.

Not this new secret, curled up inside her like a sleeping baby, that she loved him.

Certainly not the memories of how close she had been to his naked flesh in that cool water, how easy it would have been to move an inch or two closer to the line. She wondered what the salt would have tasted like on his skin, and wished she would have had the nerve to try it.

Holding that thought, she drifted, but it seemed like she had only slept a few minutes when the phone rang and startled her awake. Seven-thirty Sunday morning? Who would have the gall to be calling her at seven-thirty on Sunday morning?

Probably the cowboy had roped one too many beers at the corral last night and was still trying to round himself up a filly. The answering machine could get it.

But what if it was Abby, or even Corrine?

What if it was Mitch?

She snatched up the phone. "Hello?"

"Brit?"

It was Mitch, and even while her heart leapt at the deep, familiar pitch of his voice, his tone told her something was dreadfully wrong.

He never wanted to see her again. Her behavior last night was not what an up-and-coming lawyer wanted in a woman. He—

"I'm sorry. I woke you, didn't I? I forgot how early it is."

"What is it?" she whispered.

"Laurie asked me to call you. She said you were expecting her at the bakery today."

"She was going to get in a few extra hours getting the walls ready to repaint." She detested herself for being relieved that he had called about Laurie Rose, and not to tell her he found midnight swims in the nude completely inappropriate. "Where is she? What's happened?"

"She was arrested early this morning. In a stolen vehicle."

"Dear God. Where is she?"

"Right now in the local holding cells. She'll probably be transferred this afternoon." Brit could hear the deep sadness in his voice, overlaid with a weariness that was more than physical.

Suddenly it wasn't about *her* not wanting to be vulnerable to him. Suddenly it was about something bigger than that.

He needed her. She knew it.

"Mitch, do you want to come over? Do you need—" she almost said a shoulder to cry on, but stopped herself. "Do you need someone to talk to?"

Silence, but she heard the battle going on inside of him loud and clear.

"Yeah," he said, finally, "I do."

She put on coffee and dressed swiftly. She didn't even think about her hair. She felt sick about Laurie Rose, and she ached for Mitch.

When he arrived at her door the first thing she saw was the exhaustion in him, dark crescents under his eyes, his shoulders slumped, a heavy shadow of whiskers on his chin and cheeks.

He was the warrior come home after the battle.

And how she wanted to be the warrior's woman. To take his hands in hers, to kiss the tops of them, and then turn them over and kiss the palms, hold them to her cheeks. How she wanted to sit him down and rub the creases on his forehead, touch her fingertips to his eyelids, let her lips whisper his strength back into him.

Instead she said, "Do you want a coffee?"

"No, I just—" he reached up, ran a hand over his face.

"Come in." She did take his hand then, and led him to the couch.

He fell onto it, rested his head on the back, let his eyes shut. "I'm sorry. I haven't slept."

"Since I left you last night?"

He nodded, and she sank down on the couch beside him, hesitated and then guided the weight of his head onto her shoulder.

She ran her fingers through his hair, touched the stubble on his cheeks. "Tell me what you can," she said softly. "I know that isn't everything. I know whatever she said to you is protected by privilege."

He smiled wearily, opened his eyes, reached up and touched her cheek. "No, she asked me to tell you. Said you'd be worried about her."

So, slowly, his words thick with weariness and emotion, he told her.

"After the dance Laurie Rose bumped into a boy whom she had worshiped from afar ever since she could remember. He asked her to go for a ride with him. She was thrilled with the car, a refurbished burgundy Mustang, and of course thrilled with the attention from the boy. He'd never noticed her before."

"I should have never given her that new look," Brit moaned. "He probably would have gone on not noticing her!"

"When he'd offered her a beer, she didn't want to seem like a goody two-shoes so she took it."

"Laurie Rose!" Brit scolded, as if she was there.

"She was also understandably reluctant to tell the boy she had a court-ordered curfew. But then he didn't tell her a few things either. Like the car was stolen."

"Oh, God."

"And that he had a warrant out for his arrest on another matter."

"What on earth would she see in a boy like that?"

"You're the one who said it," he reminded her with a tired grin. "Girls adore bad boys."

"I should have talked to her about more than makeup. What was I thinking?"

"It's not your fault. I feel it, too, though, a great sense of having failed her, of having not done enough, been enough."

"Shhh," she said. "What happens to her?"

"She's in breach of her probation order because of the curfew. That's even before you start figuring in the beer, the boy and the stolen vehicle. They'll hold her in a juvenile facility until her court date.''

"What can you do?''

"Not as much as you hope and I wish. Even if she really didn't know the car was stolen—''

"And she didn't!'' Brit said fiercely.

"—the other two things don't look that great. It's not like she had a clean slate before this.''

"But can't she go home? Until her court date?''

"Brit, if she came from a good home, a supportive family who would agree to be responsible for her, maybe. But she doesn't.''

"What's the juvenile facility like?'' Brit asked, her voice shaking.

He kissed her hair. "Probably a lot nicer than her house.''

"Oh, Mitch.''

"I know,'' he said, thickly. "I know.'' And then he rested his head on her shoulder. In a short while, he was fast asleep.

And she wondered what it meant that he had come to her with his heavy heart.

She was pretty sure she knew.

It was time to ask Mitch again if he would marry her.

No holds barred this time.

None.

Mitch Hamilton wasn't going to know what hit him until after he'd marched up to the altar and said "I do.'' Because, whether he knew it or not, he needed her.

And Laurie Rose needed her.

And nobody had ever, ever needed her before, and she was not going to let them down. She slipped out from under the weight of him, laid him down gently on her couch, and covered him with a blanket.

She looked at his handsome face, relaxed in sleep, and

wondered if it was possible to love someone so much your heart could break from it.

When Mitch woke, hours later, he seemed disoriented and distant, not at all the man he had been several hours earlier. That man would have been easy to pop the question to, but the man who couldn't get off her couch and out her door fast enough was a different story.

Luckily, she had a dress fitting at Abby's. Wearing that incredible wedding gown once more cemented her feeling. She needed to get married, and she needed to do it now.

The dress carefully removed and put back on the mannequin, Brit flopped on Abby's couch. "You should have to have a license to carry those pins," she told her sister grumpily. "You're dangerous."

"What's really the matter?"

Nobody in her life had ever seen through her before as her sister did, except maybe Mitch.

Abby's house was unusually quiet. Belle was napping and Shane was working, so she poured out her heart, about the girl in jail that she needed so desperately to help, but somehow she could not even tell her own sister her secret. About loving Mitch.

"Poor kid," Abby said. "Brit, don't cry. I doubt if there's anything you can do. Mitch is probably doing his very best with a difficult situation."

"Mitch is unimaginative," Brit said. "He would never think of a solution outside of his own frame of reference."

"I don't think a career in law requires a great deal of imagination," Abby said uncertainly.

"It's just the real solution would never occur to him on his own. Never."

"The real solution?"

"Abby, what would you make for the most special dinner of your life, if you were really trying to impress someone?"

"Does this have something to do with that girl and Mitch?" Abby asked, flabbergasted about the sudden change in direction to the conversation.

"Uh, no." It would be too embarrassing to admit to her sister that she was falling back on the oldest adage known to man—or maybe that was woman—since her more modern efforts had all failed her.

Was the way to win a man through his stomach?

She intended to find out.

"Is this just theoretical?" Abby asked hopefully.

"Of course."

"Because some things are not for beginners in the kitchen."

"Never mind that part. Just tell me what you'd cook!"

"Lobster, mushroom-stuffed potatoes, fresh asparagus, homemade bread sticks, and Caesar salad. And for dessert—"

"Never mind dessert. I have enough chocolate mocha torte in the freezer at the bakery that I never have to worry about dessert again."

"I thought this was theoretical?" Abby said worriedly.

"Oh, it is."

"Because, really there are some things you might not want to try if you're not experienced."

"Like painting?" Brit asked dryly.

"Well—"

"Abby, never mind. You can't reform me. I *need* to do things the hard way."

"But why?"

"Sister, I have no idea."

Which was exactly what she was thinking two nights later, when she was looking at the lobsters in her sink, greeny colored, their huge claws banded so they wouldn't snap her fingers off, still crawling around slowly and blinking their horrible baleful black eyes at her.

It occurred to her that despite the fact they were not exactly adorable, she might have difficulties marching them off the plank into the boiling water that awaited them.

Meanwhile, Brit's kitchen looked like a bomb had gone off in it, and smelled worse. There were little bits of gluey flour stuck to the counters, mixed in with the potato goop also stuck on the counter. Her bread sticks looked like toenails that had gotten that horrible fungus she had just seen on the news, thick and twisted, and much too brown. The mushroom-stuffed potatoes had to go without the mushrooms since she had burned them right to the bottom of the pan, hence the smell.

At the moment she was trying to convince the cooked potato skins to part with their innards, so she could mash them and restuff them, but they were reluctant to get with the program. The potatoes were not cooked enough and she kept breaking through the skins with the spoon. So far, this effort looked about as appetizing as cold porridge.

The doorbell rang.

Her hair was not done, and she was not dressed.

"Just a minute," she called.

Why couldn't anything with Mitch Hamilton go according to her plan, even just once?

Sighing, she went and opened her apartment door.

Her mouth fell open. He had brought flowers. For her. Which made her think maybe her plan was not as insane as she was beginning to think it was.

He reached out and touched her face, squinted at his finger. "Flour?"

"Or maybe potato," she said dourly.

"Are *you* cooking something?"

"I invited you over for dinner. You needn't sound so surprised."

"You just don't look like that *type* of girl."

A bad sign since she was sure the type of girl a man

married cooked. And shelled peas and made jam and all
the stuff her sister did.

"What type of girl do I look like?" she shot back.

He regarded her thoughtfully and grinned. "The Yellow
Pages type," he decided. "Invite a guy for dinner, see who
delivers."

Despite the banter, she could see the somberness in his
eyes, the strain around the curve of his mouth.

"Laurie Rose?" she asked him.

"I'm working on it," he said.

She took the flowers from him and pressed her nose into
them. "I'll put them in some water. Do you want a glass
of wine or something?"

"A soda is fine, if you have it." He followed her into
the kitchen. "Wow," he finally said softly. "Do this often?"

She glared at him, tossed him the Yellow Pages and
turned her back on him while she arranged the flowers.
"You choose. Pizza or Chinese."

"Aren't we going to eat, uh, this?" He was peering at
her bread sticks.

"Not if we value our lives."

She gave a little squeal when she turned on the water in
the sink, which brought one of the lobsters rearing up at
her. She noticed she kept her grip on his flowers, though.

He was at her side and peering over her shoulder in the
blink of an eye.

"What the hell?"

"Lobster. They were going to be supper, but I can't."

"Can't what?"

"Murder them."

"Lobster? What's the occasion?"

She felt her heart quicken. "Oh, I just wanted to try
cooking. I've done so many other things I thought I'd never

do. To be honest, I thought it would be a snap. Read the directions and voilà a wonderful meal.''

"Well, I'm honored that you chose me to experiment on.''

"Seriously?''

He nodded. She thought that seemed very hopeful. Maybe he'd be honored that she had decided to try marriage on him, too. Honored.

"Do you want me to do it? Cook the lobsters?''

"I don't think so. I even named them. Billy and Buddy.''

"Naming them might have been a mistake,'' he said.

"The cookbook says to drop them in the boiling water, alive, headfirst.''

"If you leave the room, I'll do it.''

"Do you know why headfirst?''

"I can't even guess.''

"So you don't have to hear them scream.'' She shuddered.

"I don't think we'll be eating these lobsters tonight,'' he decided.

"Thank God.''

"Can I ask what you're going to do with them? I mean I don't think you want to keep them as pets. They kind of tie up your sink.''

She turned back to him, the flowers safely in a vase. "We could set them free. Take them to the ocean after we're done eating and toss them back in.''

"Free Billy,'' he said and started to laugh, and she knew everything was going to be all right.

"You want to call out? I'm going to get changed, and wash the flour off my face.''

"Don't do it for my benefit. I like you just the way you are.''

"You do?'' she breathed. She glanced down at her flour-splotched tank top and her equally stained jeans.

"I do," he said, which reminded her of the whole point of the dinner. To get Mitch to say I do.

"I'm changing," she said firmly.

When she came back out, the pizza had arrived, and she sat there in her beautiful Carmen Marc Valvo black shift, every strand of hair in place, eating with her hands on her sofa.

So nervous she could hardly think.

And not about dribbling pizza on her dress, either.

"I forgot to take dessert out of the freezer," she moaned.

"Don't worry about it. I'm not much of a dessert fan."

"A terrible thing to say to a bakery owner."

"Brit, why don't you just get it off your chest?"

"What?" she stammered.

"Something's been eating at you since the moment I walked in that door. You're not yourself. Subdued. What's up?"

She took a deep breath.

"I've given this a lot of thought Mitch."

"Okay."

"Laurie Rose needs a stable home. Isn't that what you said? That maybe they would let her out if she had a stable home to go to?"

He nodded. Did she see just a touch of wariness in his eyes?

"I don't think I'd be considered exactly a great home, now," she rushed on. "I mean a single woman, living in a one-bedroom apartment over a bakery."

"So?" he said.

"I need you. If you married me—"

She saw his face close up, and knew with panic and desperation she had lost.

He set down his pizza slowly, and looked at her.

"No."

He looked furious, but his words were measured, icy calm.

"You see, Brit, all my life people have needed me. My mom. My brothers and sister, even to a certain extent Jordan and Helen."

She stared at him, fighting tears, feeling foolish and broken.

"I guess somewhere in me I have this stupid, old-fashioned notion that I'm going to marry a girl someday for the simple reason that she loves me. And that I love her back. Is that too much to ask?"

She shook her head, wordless, the tears like fire behind her eyes as she fought to retain some scrap of dignity and not cry, not fling herself at his feet and tell him.

The irony was if she had just told him what was in her heart, just told him the simple truth, he might not be walking out that door now.

He did not glance back.

The door closed with a cold click behind him.

And then Brit threw herself down on the sofa and cried and cried and cried.

Chapter Nine

Mitch realized he was driving too fast, and eased off the gas, then slowed and pulled onto the shoulder of the highway. He got out of his car, slammed the door, and climbed the rock bluff beside him. The ocean crashed far beneath him.

He took the velvet box out of his pocket.

It felt like it had been burning a hole through his skin all night.

He'd bought the ring instead of the dog. A stupid error in judgment.

His rebel tried to soothe him, even had the nerve to ask him why he hadn't said yes. The other morning when he'd shown up at her place, and she had taken him to her couch, and run soothing hands over his brow, he felt like he'd known what was right.

Known exactly what was right for him and for her and for the rest of their lives.

He'd felt like he was finally surrendering to the pull he had felt toward her from he first moment he'd see her in his father's office, almost two whole months ago.

He'd bought the ring. She'd called. And he'd planned to ask her.

But damn her, she'd beaten him to the punch, and a bloody good thing, too.

He didn't want to marry anybody because she needed him.

To keep her damn bakery, to help Laurie Rose.

If he married that woman, he wanted it to be because she was on fire for him. Because she lay awake at night thinking of his naked body in the ocean. Because she was restless with wanting him, desperate with it.

He wanted her to marry him because she could talk to him late into the night, pour out her heart, her hopes and dreams.

He wanted her to marry him so they could laugh together.

It occurred to him there was a word for what he was thinking. He had even said it tonight. A simple word. A timeless word. The word he least wanted to think of in conjunction with Brittany Patterson right now.

He flung back his hand, the ring box in it, ready to hurl it into the sea.

But his rebel said to him, in a voice that was not quite his rebel's, a voice from yet deeper within him, "Don't throw it all away. Not yet."

He slipped the ring back into his pocket, but he did so grudgingly. Then he turned and walked away from the edge of the cliff.

So, Brit asked herself, for at least the millionth time, why hadn't she just told him the truth? When he'd said it was his heart's desire to have someone love him, why hadn't she told him that someone was her?

Because it would have seemed too contrived? Too convenient that he stated what he wanted and—presto—here she was?

No, that was not the reason at all.

Brit realized with sudden and startling clarity she was an actress. Her whole life she had put on a front—the outgoing girl—the one who knew the right dress for every occasion and could be counted on to arrive full of laughter and energy and mischief.

And it's not that that was completely false, but it simply was not completely true either.

In some ways that fun-loving, carefree persona hid a girl who longed for a mother.

Hid a girl who wanted so painfully to be loved.

Hid a girl who was afraid of her own sensitivity, so afraid of it she rarely let anyone see it.

And maybe that was the true reason she hadn't told Mitch she loved him. Because it would require her to leave the safety of the little role she was so comfortable playing, and become more.

To love Mitch would require her to be the most genuine person she could be. And the truth was she was not sure if she was ready to be that vulnerable to anyone.

No wonder people married for convenience.

None of this ripping away of masks, unveiling of deep insecurities, yearning to find that deep and wondrous place within that would be called soul.

But finding that place would require an absolute and irrevocable commitment.

"Ye gads," she said. She dug through a messy drawer in her kitchen and found an address book. Yes, there it was, right under *F*.

Farley Houser, a man who would never require her to be more than a pretty face and an enchanting smile. A man who would know the difference between Dior and Yves Saint Laurent.

A man who would never scorn Scarlett O'Hara in favor of Madam Mim.

Her fingers trembling, she dialed the number.

"Farley," she said, when he answered. "This is your future wife speaking." Her tone was light and bright, and only one person in the whole world would have heard the heartbreak underneath it.

And that was the very person who had broken her heart.

Three days later, she knocked on Abby's door. She would have done anything not to have to try on that dress once more, but how could she get out of it? How could she say the dress made her feel, acutely, the things she most didn't want to feel right now without having to answer all kinds of questions?

Instead, she pasted her brightest smile on her face.

"Guess what, sister?" she asked her as Abby opened the door.

Abby scanned her face, and didn't seem the least taken in by the bright smile. "What?" she asked cautiously.

Brit held up her hand. A huge cluster diamond glittered brightly on her engagement finger.

Abby stared at the ring, then scanned Brit's face again. "Somehow I can't see Mitch buying you a ring like that," she said, and folded her arms over her chest.

"Mitch?" She laughed scornfully. "I wouldn't marry that old sourpuss if he was the last man on earth."

"Oh, Brit!"

"Aren't you going to ask me who? Aren't you thrilled for me?" Her sister was not falling for the act that seemed harder to do than it ever had before.

"Who?" Abby asked her with monosyllabic reluctance.

"Farley Houser."

"Who?"

"He was at your wedding. A very distinguished senior

partner at Hamilton, Sweet and Hamilton. I've mentioned him to you before.''

"You don't mean that old man, do you? The one who seemed so slick?''

Brittany found herself getting annoyed. "He is not *that* old! And what do you mean slick? Charming, sophisticated, and fun-loving. Not to mention very rich.''

"Oh, Brit.''

"Don't say that again.''

"Why?''

"Because you're supposed to be happy for me. Ecstatic. Thrilled. Just the way I was for you when you told me you were going to marry Shane.''

"I loved Shane. He loved me.''

"Details,'' Brit said airily.

"It's just that you and Mitch are so obviously meant for each other. What does Mitch think of all this?''

"I don't plan to ask him, and how could he possibly be meant for me? Serious and sour and a general wet blanket.''

"He balanced you, Brit. He seemed like your opposite, but he really wasn't. He was your other half. And you were his.''

"Oh, pooh. Romantic nonsense. Tina Turner said it all. 'What's love got to do with it?' ''

"Romance is wonderful,'' her sister said stubbornly, "and love is the only thing worth living for.''

"It is not! It's upsetting. It keeps you awake at night, and makes you look in the mirror and not even know who's looking back at you.''

"Somehow I don't think Harley Fouser made you feel like that.''

"He certainly doesn't. He worships the ground I walk on, which is exactly what I'm looking for in life.''

"Is it?''

Brit thought, desperately, that the problem with having

a sister was they knew far too much, saw with more than their eyes, looked not at the smiling face that was presented to them, but at the soul that was in hiding.

Abby was looking at her and seeing her heart and soul. And the expression on Abby's face was one of such abject disappointment, as if she could see the treachery Brit was committing against her own heart.

Brit felt sick inside. She had disappointed her sister.

Well, wasn't it just a matter of time before she did that to everyone?

"Lighten up, Abby. You're supposed to be happy for me. Thrilled."

"So you've said." Abby looked like she was going to burst into tears. The doorbell rang. "I don't even want to get that. I don't want to talk to anyone right now."

"You'd think I had just announced a funeral instead of a wedding. Don't be ridiculous," Brit said, and opened the door. "Oh, Mrs. Pondergrove, how are you?"

"Abby?"

Brit laughed, and it sounded brittle and high-strung, even to her. "No. Come in." She welcomed this diversion from her sister's intensely discomforting scrutiny.

"I don't want to interrupt. I just came to see about the dress."

"It's nearly done, Angela," Abby said. "Brit was just going to try it on, one last time. Do you want to see it?"

"Oh, could I? If it's not too much trouble?"

"I'd be happy to model it for you," Brit said, though nothing could be further from the truth. "In fact, I'm going to be a bride soon myself. Nothing fancy though. A night or two in Las Vegas. My Chanel will do nicely."

"You're getting married, dear?" Mrs. Pondergrove asked, her whole face lighting up. "This must be brand new. Jordan hasn't breathed a word to me."

"She's not marrying Mitch," Abby said grouchily.

"What? But he seems so," her voice trailed away, and she looked at Brit baffled and hurt somehow, "perfect."

Brit thought this was definitely a problem with small towns. Everyone knew everything about everybody. Or thought they did.

"I'm marrying Farley Houser," she said proudly. "We're going to fly to Vegas on the weekend."

"Vegas?" Mrs. Pondergrove breathed with horror. "Mr. Houser? Isn't he that older gentleman that works with Jordan?"

"Distinguished," Brit corrected her, through gritted teeth.

"Distinguished," Mrs. Pondergrove repeated, unconvinced. "Oh, dear. Oh, dear me."

Brit stared at the little old lady, nonplussed, then glanced at Abby. The lady hardly knew her. What was the cause of all this distress?

Abby met her eyes over Mrs. Pondergrove's shoulder, and shrugged. "Angela, let me get you a nice cup of tea, while Brit tries on the dress."

"Yes, a cup of tea would be nice."

Brit took the dress off the mannequin, a little more roughly than she should have. She would try on the dress, and do a few twirls. What she wouldn't do was even glance at herself in the mirror. Not even one little glance.

She went and put on the dress, her back determinedly to the mirror. Childishly, she closed her eyes the whole time she was slipping it on. It barely helped. The fabric whispered against her skin. She began to hum so she would not hear the name it was whispering.

Act, she ordered herself, when it felt like she might cry.

She pretended she was a model, tilted her chin way up, kept a look of regal coolness on her face, as she swept into the kitchen. No one ever knew what those models were thinking under all that remote hauteur. She avoided eye contact with her audience of two.

She had no desire to see the dreams the dress would bring to their eyes.

She pretended she was in Paris, and that it was just another gown, and she had fifty more to try on before she was done her runway duty for the day. With a final pirouette she swept out of the room.

She could hear the murmur of their voices behind her.

And they weren't applauding either.

Brit was sure she could hear disapproval. Oh, what else was new? Everyone always disapproved of her.

After hanging the dress back up, she came into the kitchen.

"Well, I must go," she said brightly. "I have a million things to do."

"Angela has something she wants to say to you," Abby said in a low voice.

"My dear, I want you to have the dress."

Brit's mouth fell open. "That dress? Me?"

"Yes. I'd like you to have it as a gift."

"I couldn't possibly accept it," Brit said vehemently. "It's not going to be that kind of wedding."

Mrs. Pondergrove looked bewildered. "The dress looked lovely on you. Like a vision. How could any woman not want to look like that on her own wedding day?"

"I just don't," Brit said firmly.

Mrs. Pondergrove sighed heavily. "I insist, my dear. Take the dress. Do what you choose with it."

"You don't even know me! You can't give away a dress like that to a complete stranger."

Mrs. Pondergrove's nose became very pinched, and then she said, her voice soft and broken. "We are not as much strangers as you think. I—I knew your mother."

Brit saw Abby's mouth fall open, and knew hers must have done the same thing.

"You knew our mother?" she whispered.

Mrs. Pondergrove's distress seemed to be growing. "Briefly. I'm sorry. It's a long story, and a complicated one."

"What she was like?" Brit breathed. "Was she beautiful, and gentle? Did she love me? Us?"

"Did she love you? Oh, my dear." And then Mrs. Pondergrove was weeping. "Of course she loved you. I have to leave. I have to go now. I'm so sorry." She tottered to her feet.

And then obviously deeply distressed, she picked up her purse and toddled toward the door.

"Mrs. Pondergrove," Brit cried, "Please don't leave so upset." What she wanted to say was *please don't leave until I know everything about my mother.*

"I'll be fine, dear. Just fine." She dabbed under her glasses at her eyes, and then she was gone, like a thin wisp of gray smoke.

Brit and Abby stared at each other.

"She knew our mom," Abby said slowly.

"I wonder what she was so sorry about?" Brit asked.

"Ha," Abby said. "No question, there. Your upcoming wedding."

Brit stuck her tongue out at her sister. "And I don't want that dress."

"Why not?" Abby asked innocently.

"Because," Brit said, "I hate it, and I hate everything it stands for."

Abby looked at her sadly and shook her head.

Mitch didn't look up when his office door opened. "What?" he growled.

"I've been appointed to come get a donation from you," Millie said sternly. "Suzie was scared to come do it."

"Scared?" Mitch said, glancing up. "Of me?"

"Oh for heaven's sake, don't act the innocent. You've been an absolute horror. You made her cry yesterday."

"I did?"

"It was just a typing error. One digit out."

"On an address!"

"Mr. Hamilton!"

"I need to apologize?"

"If we are going to have any secretaries left at the end of the week, you do. And—" she shook the large can she was holding in his face, "your amends could start with a substantial donation."

He fished for his wallet. "For what?"

"Mr. Houser is getting married again. Suzie's in charge of the office party. She wants to try the new place. Yoko's House of Fine Curry. It's the talk of the town, but I'm not so sure about it. What kind of name is that for a restaurant? Curry isn't Japanese, is it? And she thought a patio set for a gift. Mr. Houser has that big deck on his condo—"

Mitch felt like he was frozen. He had lost Millie somewhere around the word curry. His hand froze on its way to his wallet, his voice felt like it was frozen in his throat.

"Who?" he asked, knowing he failed to sound casual, his voice feeling like he was chipping the ice away to allow the sound to come out.

"Suzie." Millie was looking at him like he was the class dunce.

"He's marrying Suzie?" Relief, pouring through him, the blood beginning to move in his veins again, slowly, sluggishly.

"Mr. Hamilton! Suzie's very happily married. She's in charge of the office party and getting the gift."

He asked it very slowly, enunciating each word so that

there was no possible way he could be misunderstood. "Who...is...Farley...marrying?"

"Oh. One of those lovely triplets who was in here not very long ago. Of course, everyone's saying she's too young for him, but the man is smitten. I've never seen him happier. He looks ten years younger than he did last week. Mr. Hamilton? Where are you going? Mr. Hamilton!"

He felt like the blood was pounding in his head. The rebel was out, and he had come out swinging.

Mitch covered the distance between his office and Farley's in under a second. He threw open the door and went in without knocking.

"If you marry her," he said softly, his breath heaving in his chest, "I'm going to kill you with my bare hands."

He could not believe he had said that. Nor could he believe how strongly he meant it.

Farley stared at him, astonished, his pen paralyzed above his legal pad. He regained his composure quickly. "Did you want to sit down?" he said, with an edge of sarcasm.

"No."

"She asked me," he said smoothly. "Only a complete fool would have said no."

Mitch folded his arms over his chest and narrowed his eyes.

"You had your chance," Farley said with a shrug.

"How do you know?"

"She told me."

He hated that. That she had told him things. Confided in Farley. That they had spent time together. Maybe even alone. Had Farley kissed her?

Maybe he wouldn't wait to kill him. Maybe he'd leap across that desk, and grab him by his tie and start to twist....

"Mitch, don't look at me like that. You said no. What would you do? Send her off to the nunnery? Are you trying to tell me, in your subtle way, that you think there's still something between you?''

So, he stood at the edge of the cliff again. He had to leap or back off. Backing off had brought him absolutely no peace. Backing off had been eating him alive for days.

''Yes,'' he said, ''there's something between us.''

Farley looked at him long and hard, folded his arms over his chest. ''Then you should have said yes. Why the hell didn't you?''

''She asked me for all the wrong reasons.''

''Such as?''

''Look, Farley, given your history you might not get this, but I have this old-fashioned need to be loved by the woman I marry.''

''You know, Mitch, I'll be straight with you. If it's all about what you need, you don't deserve her. Have you ever asked yourself what the hell she needs?''

Mitch stared at him, stunned.

The simple answer was no, he hadn't done that. And now that he had he knew two things that weren't true.

She didn't need that bakery. And she didn't need Laurie Rose.

Suddenly he pictured her as a little girl, in her pretty dresses, dying to be loved for something other than being pretty. He thought of her need to look so perfect and about that bright smile she manufactured that didn't always reach her eyes.

And he knew what she needed.

Just like that.

And he knew he was the only man alive that could give it to her.

''Too young for me,'' Farley decided sadly. ''I mean I knew that, but a man hopes.'' He was watching Mitch. ''Do you love her, son?'' he asked softly.

Suddenly the fury was gone, just like that. Mitch

slumped into a chair in front of Farley's desk and nodded.
"Yeah."

"Stupid young pup."

He glared up at the older man.

"Do you understand how rare that is?" Farley said, not
cowed, his eyes blazing. "Are you going to throw that
away? Over some point of pride?"

"No," Mitch said, his voice suddenly as strong as his
determination. "No, I'm not."

Sighing, Farley reached into the inside pocket of his suit
jacket and withdrew two slender envelopes, unmistakably
airline tickets.

"Here," he said. "You have these. I won't be needing
them now."

Mitch took the tickets. Las Vegas. This weekend. He felt
the earth shifting around him at how close he had come to
throwing it all away.

Farley picked up his phone, tucked the mouthpiece into
his chest. "If you make her unhappy, I'll kill you. With
my bare hands." He looked quite pleased with himself.
And then he lifted the mouthpiece, and said, "Sam? How
are you? Look on this Williamson deal—"

He did not look at Mitch, twirled his chair around so he
faced his windows.

And Mitch knew the decent thing to do, the only thing
to do, would be to leave quietly, and not destroy Farley's
composure entirely by thanking him for the gift he had just
been given.

Chapter Ten

As far as days went, Brit thought, it had been a good day.

Luigi, the baker, crushed when she had told him about Laurie Rose's problems, had actually scolded her when she'd told him her solution.

"You're notta marrying thatta man. He isa not for you."

"Oh, what difference does it make who you marry?" she said. "What's everyone got against Farley? He's such a nice man."

Luigi had scowled at her.

And Brit had been utterly disgusted with herself. Even Luigi seemed to see right through her, now.

Clucking away he had spent the rest of the day on the phone, speaking rapid-fire and passionate Italian. But at the end of the day, he'd informed her he had talked it over with his wife, and if Laurie Rose needed a place to stay she could stay with them. They had an appointment with a social worker to discuss it further.

"Whatsa one more?" he said. "We have nine already. My middle daughter Salina is about Laurie's age. So they share a room."

"Nine children?" Brit breathed.

He snorted. "And you ask *me* what difference it makes who you marry. You marry someone who sets your heart on fire, thatsa what."

So, Laurie's problems were closer to resolution, without any drastic action on her part. Add to that the fact she was getting better at figuring out receipts at the end of the day, and today they were actually in the black, and they were only halfway through the week.

Which meant when she went shopping after work she splurged on a wonderful barbecued chicken, and didn't even go down the tuna aisle.

But best of all, instead of things going back to chaos with Laurie Rose being away, Brit found she coped. Certainly things were not going quite as smoothly as when her young assistant was mopping and polishing everything in sight, but they had not fallen apart, either.

And she had managed to get through a whole day without thinking about her upcoming wedding.

Still, if life was so good, she had to ask herself what she was doing in bed at seven o'clock at night, in flannelette pajamas, which she had never worn in her entire life, and feeling like she had a hangover, when she hadn't had a thing to drink since her sister's wedding?

The truth, which she was trying with all her might to outrun, was her heart was broken.

Farley knew the truth. He had known it all along, somehow seen through her bright talk just like everyone else and gotten it out of her. That she was marrying him on the rebound. To meet a condition for a gift. To help a kid in need.

Brit thought she was being unfair to Farley, but if he didn't think so, then was it still unfair? The type of question that drove her crazy, kept her up until all hours of the night, made her hand people a loaf of bread when they had just asked for a doughnut and a coffee.

Once upon a time, when she had wanted to keep her real feelings to herself, she'd been able to do that. Nobody had ever seen through her before.

And now everybody could.

And now that the Laurie Rose issue had another solution, were she and Farley still going to forge ahead?

Bang. Bang. Bang.

She didn't want to open the door. She pulled the pillow over her head. But whoever was out there would not go away.

Finally, not even bothering with her housecoat, she went and threw open the door.

A delivery boy stood there, a big square box in his hands. She knew immediately what it was. "I don't want that," she said.

But it seemed even he could see through her.

"Lady, I get paid for deliveries. Extra at this time of night. So just sign your name here, and take the box. Why make my life difficult? Throw it over the railing after, for all I care. I bet you could hit that Dumpster from here."

She glared at him but he seemed unperturbed. He handed her a pen and huffily she took it and signed her name. He thrust the box into her arms, and went back down her stairs. He glanced back once.

She had the feeling he had known she wasn't going to throw the box off the landing and into the Dumpster.

In another lifetime, before she knew what a privilege it was to eat barbecued chicken instead of tuna, she might have.

The damned problem was now she couldn't even lie to herself. Her not throwing that box off the edge of her landing and into the nearest Dumpster had nothing to do with the price of the item inside. Nothing to do with her sister's hours and hours of painstaking labor.

She took the box and put it in the middle of her kitchen table. Deliberately, and with great pleasure in her self-control, she turned her back from it and plugged in the kettle.

See? It had no power over her.

After the kettle was plugged in, she took down a coffee mug and stirred four tablespoons of instant coffee into it before adding the water. It wasn't until she sipped that she admitted maybe the contents of that box had a wee sway over her.

She slid it a little look, sorted through her mail without registering a single item, then slid it another look. She walked around her table three times not once even touching it.

And then furious with herself for her utter lack of self-control she grabbed the box, ripped the brown paper off it and flipped up the lid.

Folded carefully in a bed of tissue was the dress. It seemed to glow from within it was so beautiful and so full of magic. She reached in and touched it, closed her eyes at the delicacy of the fabric beneath her fingertips, then opened her eyes again.

On top of the dress was a piece of folded notepaper, and she reached for it with trembling hands, and opened it.

The handwriting was so frail it looked like cobwebs.

My dearest Brittany,

   I am so sorry for my behavior the other night, and for surprising you with the news I knew your mother. My meeting with her was a brief and tragic one. I had hoped to tell you, and your sisters about it when the time seemed right. Now I have decided I must go away for a while. I feel confused and unsure, though I still hold one truth.

   There is only one reality and one power. It is love.

I beg you not to choose anything less for yourself. I beg you. Your mother would have asked nothing less.

                                        Angela Pondergrove.

Somehow the words crept over her, caught her in a grip that the frail writing belied. *I beg you. Your mother would have asked nothing less.*

After a long time, Brit set the note aside, and ran her fingers over the dress, caressed it. There was something soothing about stroking it with a tender, reverent touch.

"I won't try it on," she told herself. But she looked at her coffee cup and her mail, and even when she ordered them to, her feet would not move away from the dress and toward other more reasonable activities.

She gave in. She scooped the dress out of the box, and shook it gently, and it unfolded in front of her.

"If I try this dress on," she said shakily, out loud, "I won't ever marry Farley Houser."

She had told him she would. It was only days away. Good grief, she had told most of the town she was so intent on convincing herself it was all right.

Or maybe it was because she was so intent on word getting back to Mitch.

Silence from Mitch.

And if Mitch wasn't going to marry her, then it really didn't matter who she married, did it?

As if in a trance, she undid the snap on her jeans and let them slide off of her hips and onto the floor. Holding the dress with one hand, she undid the buttons of her blouse with the other and then tugged it off and let it fall beside the jeans.

But how could she not try it on, just one more time?

And see herself as she was meant to be.

She took the dress, and with awe she slid it over her shoulders, felt its scant weight settle over her, and fall into place. She reached behind her, and as she pulled up the back zipper, the dress came to life, and hugged her, clung to her, like a second skin.

Helpless, she allowed herself to fall further into its spell. A rich contentment came over her. She curtsied to an imaginary groom, laughed into his eyes, then she turned on Celine Dion and began to do an imaginary waltz around the room with him.

She knew she was never going to marry Farley Houser.

It didn't matter if she lost the bakery, and she would find another way to help Laurie Rose, even if Luigi's rescue fell through.

How right Angela had been. Only one thing was real, only one thing had any power.

And she danced with it.

She danced with the girl who had become a woman in the last few weeks. Who had learned to run a bakery, against impossible odds, and who knew how to buy her own groceries and clean up her own puddles and messes and mistakes.

It was that woman who had fallen in love with Mitch Hamilton.

The girl who thought, only moments ago, that she could marry Farley Houser, faded and grew more shadowy by the second until she was smoke and then mist and then she no longer existed. And as that girl faded, a woman stepped up and took her place.

A real woman. Strong and resourceful, creative and compassionate. A woman completely able to look after herself.

And then Brit knew that was why she had come to Miracle Harbor. Not to claim a bakery, not to get married, but to lay claim to the miracle within herself.

And someday there would be a man big enough to love that *real* woman. She knew that with certainty. There would be a wedding someday. And not because she *had* to have one. She would save this dress for that day, the day she got married because she wanted to.

Because she was on fire for a man, because love could make her even more than she was in this moment.

He came to her mind. The man that she wished it would be, and the tears came finally and trickled down her cheeks, though she danced on.

A knock on the door.

She realized she'd forgotten to give the delivery boy a tip, not that he'd deserved one. She turned up the music, ignored him hammering on the door.

"Brit, if you don't open this door, I'm going to break it down."

She realized, all along, she had known Mitch would come. Everyone had known. Her sister and Mrs. Pondergrove and Luigi, and even Farley.

Some truths were too strong to hide.

Yes, from the minute she had put on the dress she had known all things were possible.

She went to the door. And opened it.

He stood there, his hair disheveled and his cheeks shadowed by dark whiskers, some agony in his eyes.

He looked at her, but she was certain he didn't even see that dress.

All he saw was what Mitch had always seen. Her. The real her.

He stepped toward her, and when she matched his step and moved toward him, he sighed and came yet closer, until finally he could lay his head on her shoulder.

Her warrior. Home from his battles. For good.

She put her arms around him, pulled herself in tighter to him, murmured his name over and over like a mantra that brought peace and strength. She felt him relax against her, felt the part of him he had never given before come to her willingly.

His trust. She looked into his eyes, and smiled her welcome, and he whispered her name and kissed the hollow of her throat, and then the crest of her cheekbones and the soft flesh of her closed eyes.

"Brit," he said. "I'm so sorry. Forgive me."

"For?" she asked softly.

"For not saying yes. For not recognizing what you couldn't say, but what anyone but a blind man could have seen."

"And what was that?"

"That you loved me."

Her final secret gone, torn so tenderly from her. And yet stepping out from behind the shield of that secret, Brit Patterson felt as free as she had ever felt, like she had wings and could soar with eagles.

"Yes," she said. "I love you."

"And here is my secret. Brit, I love you, too. Maybe from that first moment in my father's office I recognized your soul as the one that would set my soul free. Bring light into my world, after I have walked so long in darkness, bring laughter to my heart when I had given up believing there were things that could be so joyful."

"Mitch—"

"I'm not done. I have a confession to make. I told Farley Houser today if you married him I would kill him with my bare hands."

"The rebel steps forward," she said.

"It wasn't my right to do that, Brit. It was wrong—"

"Shhh. We both knew I was never marrying Farley. Everybody knew, including him. You and I just knew last. How could I marry him, Mitch, when I'm so in love with you? How could I have ever lived with such a monstrous lie? How could I have even considered it?"

He stared at her, looked deep into her eyes. A smile like she had never seen came to his lips, warmed his entire face, made his eyes dance with the most incredible light.

And then she was smiling, too, and it felt like her whole life had been a desert that she crossed to reach this one moment, to prove herself worthy of this one moment.

When everything made sense, and everything was exactly as it was meant to be.

"Do you want to go to Las Vegas and get married this weekend? I've come into a couple of tickets," he said.

"No." Firmly.

He put her away from him, lifted that one eyebrow.

She smoothed it down with her finger.

"We're getting married right here. I have the place all picked out. It's called Hope. Those kids would never forgive us if they weren't invited to your wedding."

"You want to get married at the teen center?"

"I can't wait."

"I don't exactly think your parents are going to approve of the neighborhood."

"I've been doing some serious growing up, lately. It doesn't really matter to me if they approve or not. In fact, I think they might have something to learn there."

"And what's that?"

"That love makes miracles happen. All the time. Anywhere it's given a chance it takes root, and miracles begin to happen."

"Miracles," he agreed, and caught her lips with his, and intertwined his hand in hers, and to the soaring notes of a love song they took the first steps of the rest of their lives.

With their hearts and their lips and their souls, they said yes to the greatest miracle of all.

One man, one woman, loving each other for all time, allowing that love to heal in them all places broken, and to fill in them all places empty.

* * * * *

THE WEDDING LEGACY
*continues next month
with Corrine's story!
Look for*

WED BY A WILL

*by Cara Colter
(Silhouette Romance 1544)*

Here's a sneak preview...

Chapter One

Hers.

Corrine shoved her hands in the back pockets of her jeans and rocked back and forth on her heels, studying the cabin. It stood, small and solid, under the spreading wings of a giant maple tree.

Hers.

She sighed, and allowed herself to feel a little finger of happiness. Nothing had ever really been hers before.

Maybe it would be tempting fate to believe that good things could happen to her. Nothing in her history allowed her to believe good things lasted.

"Well," she said out loud, and smiled, "according to my sister Brit, this place doesn't qualify as a good thing. Not even close."

Brit had been appalled by the tiny cabin, the tumbledown barn, the falling down fences.

"You can come live with me and Mitch," Brit had announced.

"You're newlyweds!" Cory had said. Her sister had

been married for only a week. She and her husband, Mitch, had hardly been able to keep their hands off each other long enough to say the vows. Cory didn't want to live with that—cold, hard evidence, that dreams came true, that miracles happened all the time.

Both her sisters were evidence of that, judging by the happiness they had found since coming to Miracle Harbor. The thought of finding that kind of happiness for herself made terror claw in Cory's throat.

Never cry, had always been Cory's first rule. But the second rule was just as strong: *don't hold hope*. Having hope could be the most dangerous thing of all.

She took a deep breath, and glanced around.

There was work everywhere. The barn was practically falling down. The yard was nonexistent. Taking another deep breath, she gave the door a shove. It squeaked open.

The interior of the cabin was simplicity itself. She liked its rough-hewn gray log walls, and the window, french-paned and huge. A single beam of sunshine found its way through the grime and danced across the floor.

Lost in thought, picturing bright, yellow-checked curtains at the windows, throw rugs on the floor, red tulips in a glass jar on the kitchen table, she did not hear him come in.

"Anybody here?"

She whirled around, gasping.

The light poured through the door behind him, and for a moment all she saw was his silhouette. As she studied him, she felt herself relax minutely.

Beige cowboy hat, white T-shirt, narrow-legged jeans on long, long legs, booted feet and broad, broad shoulders. Even without the hat, something would have whispered cowboy.

Her eyes adjusted to the light and the details of him came clear to her. Brown eyes, steady, unwavering, calm and strong. His cheekbones were pronounced and his nose looked like it might have been straight once. He had a beautiful mouth.

He took a step toward her, his hand extended, and she backed up.

He lowered the hand slowly and regarded her, the eyes narrow now, assessing.

Rule Three: Never let them see your fear. It didn't matter that she didn't know why she was scared, why her heart was pumping rabbit-swift, and why everything in her knew the scariest thing she could have done was to accept that extended hand.

She knew exactly what it would feel like.

It would be warm, dry, infinitely strong, and leather-tough. The touch of that hand would invite her to look into a world where people were not alone. Just a tantalizing glimpse, before he released his grip.

A sudden yearning leapt in her that she had to fight. A yearning that made an entirely different kind of fear breathe to life inside her.

"What can I do for you?" she asked, her voice ice cold, not a trace of emotion to be heard in it.

She knew he heard the coldness, though his reaction was barely discernible. A flicker of muscle along the line of his jaw, a slight narrowing of his eyes.

"I'm Matt Donahue," he said, with just the faintest hint of ice that added a raw edge to the warm timbre of his voice. "I'm your closest neighbor," he said, nodding, "on that side."

If he expected the welcome neighbor routine, she hoped to disappoint him. She said nothing and waited.

"I actually was interested in buying this piece of land. I heard someone bought it before I even realized it had come up on the market."

So he wasn't exactly here as part of the welcome neighbor routine. Surprise, surprise.

"I'm not selling." See? That was what attachment did. She'd only just got here, and already she had decided the place was hers. A place where her heart could be at home. She felt inordinately angry at him for making her see how fragile places for the heart were.

"You haven't even heard my offer," he said mildly.

"Nor do I plan to." The land wasn't really even hers to sell, yet. And maybe it never would be. How had her heart managed to overlook that one detail of her inheritance when she was planning throw rugs and curtains and bright red tulips?

That while her heart was saying *forever* to this little shack in the trees, the legal document said something else.

Husband required.

For a moment having the "h" word in her mind at the same time that this big, handsome man with the strong, steady eyes filled her door well made her almost helpless with longing.

Wishing she could be a different person than she was. Softer and kinder, like her sister, Abby, or more outgoing and sexy like her sister, Brit.

Wishing she was not so afraid to hope that this land, even someone as extraordinary as this man, could be all hers....

*   *   *   *   *

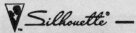

**Separated at birth,
reunited by a mysterious bequest,
these triplet sisters discover
a legacy of love!**

THE WEDDING LEGACY

A brand-new series coming to
Silhouette Romance from heartwarming author

CARA COLTER

Available July 2001:
HUSBAND BY INHERITANCE (SR #1532)

Available August 2001:
THE HEIRESS TAKES A HUSBAND (SR #1538)

Available September 2001:
WED BY A WILL (SR #1544)

Available at your favorite retail outlet.

Silhouette®
Where love comes alive™

Visit Silhouette at www.eHarlequin.com   SRTWL

Feel like a star with Silhouette.

We will fly you and a guest to New York City for an exciting weekend stay at a glamorous 5-star hotel. Experience a refreshing day at one of New York's trendiest spas and have your photo taken by a professional. Plus, receive $1,000 U.S. spending money!

Flowers...long walks...dinner for two... how does Silhouette Books make romance come alive for you?

Send us a script, with 500 words or less, along with visuals (only drawings, magazine cutouts or photographs or combination thereof). Show us how Silhouette Makes Your Love Come Alive. Be creative and have fun. No purchase necessary. All entries must be clearly marked with your name, address and telephone number. All entries will become property of Silhouette and are not returnable. **Contest closes September 28, 2001.**

Please send your entry to: **Silhouette Makes You a Star!**

In U.S.A.
P.O. Box 9069
Buffalo, NY, 14269-9069

In Canada
P.O. Box 637
Fort Erie, ON, L2A 5X3

Look for contest details on the next page, by visiting www.eHarlequin.com or request a copy by sending a self-addressed envelope to the applicable address above. Contest open to Canadian and U.S. residents who are 18 or over. Void where prohibited.

Our lucky winner's photo will appear in a Silhouette ad. Join the fun!

HARLEQUIN "SILHOUETTE MAKES YOU A STAR!" CONTEST 1308
OFFICIAL RULES
NO PURCHASE NECESSARY TO ENTER

1. To enter, follow directions published in the offer to which you are responding. Contest begins June 1, 2001, and ends on September 28, 2001. Entries must be postmarked by September 28, 2001, and received by October 5, 2001. Enter by hand-printing (or typing) on an 8 ½" x 11" piece of paper your name, address (including zip code), contest number/name and attaching a script containing 500 words or less, <u>along with drawings, photographs or magazine cutouts, or combinations thereof</u> (i.e., collage) on no larger than 9" x 12" piece of paper, describing how the <u>Silhouette books make romance come alive for you</u>. Mail via first-class mail to: Harlequin "Silhouette Makes You a Star!" Contest 1308, (in the U.S.) P.O. Box 9069, Buffalo, NY 14269-9069, (in Canada) P.O. Box 637, Fort Erie, Ontario, Canada L2A 5X3. Limit one entry per person, household or organization.

2. Contests will be judged by a panel of members of the Harlequin editorial, marketing and public relations staff. Fifty percent of criteria will be judged against script and fifty percent will be judged against drawing, photographs and/or magazine cutouts. Judging criteria will be based on the following:

   - Sincerity—25%
   - Originality and Creativity—50%
   - Emotionally Compelling—25%

   In the event of a tie, duplicate prizes will be awarded. Decisions of the judges are final.

3. All entries become the property of Torstar Corp. and may be used for future promotional purposes. Entries will not be returned. No responsibility is assumed for lost, late, illegible, incomplete, inaccurate, nondelivered or misdirected mail.

4. Contest open only to residents of the U.S. (except Puerto Rico) and Canada who are 18 years of age or older, and is void wherever prohibited by law; all applicable laws and regulations apply. Any litigation within the Province of Quebec respecting the conduct or organization of a publicity contest may be submitted to the Régie des alcools, des courses et des jeux for a ruling. Any litigation respecting the awarding of a prize may be submitted to the Régie des alcools, des courses et des jeux only for the purpose of helping the parties reach a settlement. Employees and immediate family members of Torstar Corp. and D. L. Blair, Inc., their affiliates, subsidiaries and all other agencies, entities and persons connected with the use, marketing or conduct of this contest are not eligible to enter. Taxes on prizes are the sole responsibility of the winner. Acceptance of any prize offered constitutes permission to use winner's name, photograph or other likeness for the purposes of advertising, trade and promotion on behalf of Torstar Corp., its affiliates and subsidiaries without further compensation to the winner, unless prohibited by law.

5. Winner will be determined no later than November 30, 2001, and will be notified by mail. Winner will be required to sign and return an Affidavit of Eligibility/Release of Liability/Publicity Release form within 15 days after winner notification. Noncompliance within that time period may result in disqualification and an alternative winner may be selected. All travelers must execute a Release of Liability prior to ticketing and must possess required travel documents (e.g., passport, photo ID) where applicable. Trip must be booked by December 31, 2001, and completed within one year of notification. No substitution of prize permitted by winner. Torstar Corp. and D. L. Blair, Inc., their parents, affiliates and subsidiaries are not responsible for errors in printing of contest, entries and/or game pieces. In the event of printing or other errors that may result in unintended prize values or duplication of prizes, all affected game pieces or entries shall be null and void. **Purchase or acceptance of a product offer does not improve your chances of winning.**

6. Prizes: (1) Grand Prize—A 2-night/3-day trip for two (2) to New York City, including round-trip coach air transportation nearest winner's home and hotel accommodations (double occupancy) at The Plaza Hotel, a glamorous afternoon makeover at <u>a trendy New York spa</u>, $1,000 in U.S. spending money and an opportunity to <u>have a professional photo taken and appear in a Silhouette advertisement</u> (approximate retail value: $7,000). (10) Ten Runner-Up Prizes of gift packages (retail value $50 ea.). Prizes consist of only those items listed as part of the prize. Limit one prize per person. Prize is valued in U.S. currency.

7. For the name of the winner (available after December 31, 2001) send a self-addressed, stamped envelope to: Harlequin "Silhouette Makes You a Star!" Contest 1197 Winners, P.O. Box 4200 Blair, NE 68009-4200 or you may access the www.eHarlequin.com Web site through February 28, 2002.

Contest sponsored by Torstar Corp., P.O. Box 9042, Buffalo, NY 14269-9042.

SRMYAS2

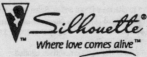